Fresh Starts, D

FRESH START, DIRTY MONEY

Lynda Rees

Fresh Starts, Dirty Money

FRESH START, DIRTY MONEY

Lynda Rees

Email: lyndareesauthor@gmail.com
Website: www.lyndareesauthor.com
Original Edition
ISBN: 978-1-960763-18-1
Copyright © 2023 by
Publisher:
Sweetwater Publishing Company
6612 Ky. Hwy. 17 North,
DeMossville, KY 41033
www.sweetwaterpublishingcompany.wordpress.com

Email: lyndareesauthor@gmail.com
Website: http://www.lyndareesauthor.com
Facebook: @lynda.rees.author

DEDICATION:

I dedicate this story to my
amazing granddaughter,
Harley S. Nelson
Thank you for blessing me with
the gift of having you in my life.
If you ever feel inadequate,
unworthy, or unloved,
remember.
You are special.
Straighten your crown.
Hold your head high.
My love for you
is eternal.

MamMa
Lynda Rees

CHAPTER ONE

Bree Collins' navigated morning rush hour traffic worse than she'd ever seen before. Even at their most snarled, Hazard traffic jams cleared up quickly. Hopefully, this wasn't the norm. Bye-bye, small town. Hello big city troubles.

The day had started with excitement for a fresh start in life. As miles dwindled away over the over-three-hour drive, thrill melted to anxiousness, to self-doubt and fear. Could she make it in a new job, a new industry, and in a new city where she knew only one person?

She turned the last corner, advised by her Bitch in the Box; and a huge shopping mall came into view. Good thing it wasn't farther from the expressway.

She would be lucky to make it by lunchtime if she had to fight this kind of traffic much longer.

Cam sputtered then stalled. The radio died. What the hell? This was completely unlike her dependable Toyota®. No matter the old girl was sporting over a hundred-thousand miles. The mechanic back home had assured Bree Cam should get over two-hundred-thousand miles in a lifetime, long as she kept the fluids up to date. She'd been meticulous when it came to car-care, sticking to a strict schedule for maintenance; and she's had Cam checked before hitting the road.

"Come on girl. We just have to make it into the parking facility. It's right there, less than a half a block away." She stroked the steering wheel. Cam completely ignored her. She twisted the key.

Nothing.

Again. Nothing.

Again. Nothing.

Horns blared behind her. Drivers gave her the middle-finger and spat obscenities she read on their angry lips as they struggled to get around her. All she could do was shrug and ignore them. She reached for her phone to call Aunt Mya but laid it back in the top of her handbag as a police cruiser pulled to stop beside her.

A darkly handsome, square-jawed police officer with a tint of gray around the sideburns rolled down his passenger window and motioned for her to do the same. She tried, but the windows didn't budge. Apparently, when Cam's engine went on the fritz, so did her electronically controlled devices.

She winced toward the cop and shrugged with a shake of her head. His eyes rolled upward. Lips pursed with a clench of his jaw, and his head shook. He rolled his window back up and threw an arm across the back of his seat. With a wave backward, he signaled the driver behind him to back up—not an easy task given the tightly clogged lane. The man backed up and signaled the guy behind him to do so. Bit-by-bit they made way for the black-and-white to move backward then pull in behind Cam.

In her rearview mirror the policeman spoke to someone on a hand radio. Then he stepped out of his car, all six-foot-several-inches of him. Tall and muscular, he rolled broad shoulders back, as though relieving tension. Thumbs in utility belt, he strode toward her door like he owned the road. He pointed, indicating she should open her door.

His thick hand clasped the door when it was about four inches wide. "That's far enough. Stay in your vehicle. Not safe out here." He glanced over his shoulder as cars moved past. "We don't want to block the flow any worse than you've already done. Got to say, you have great timing. This is the busiest time of day."

His gruff tone prickled hairs on the back of her neck, and she flinched. "It's not my fault. Cam didn't mean to ruin your day. This is totally unlike her. It's not as though we're obstructing the road on purpose."

"Cam?" His left brow shot high, but he didn't laugh or smile. "Well, we'll see. Won't we."

She held up her phone. "I was just about to call my aunt. I'm supposed to meet her here. I'm new to the area, and she could help me find a mechanic or tow truck."

"No need. I called a wrecker. He should be here in a couple minutes. You're going to be a little for your shopping excursion."

The pompous ass's attitude sent goose bumps crawling up her arms.

Who did he think he was?

He leaned toward the open door, and his chest came into view. On the right side of his thick chest a gold name badge read Rex Ayers. "At least, no one will ram into your rear end."

She swallowed the urge to spit some argument at him and gave him the sweetest smile she could muster. "She just quit. No warning or anything. When I tried over and over to restart Cam, there's a click of the starter but nothing happens." Hopefully, she didn't sound like too big of a ditz. This fella already acted like he thought she was irresponsible.

His head rocked up and down. "Sounds like the engine might be blown. That's usually because of a lack of oil. Perhaps you forgot to check the oil level in . . . Cam." He seemed to be biting his tongue, probably to avoid laughing out loud. "You know, I should give you a ticket for impeding traffic."

Before she could bite her lip, anger took control of her tongue. "I'll have you know—"

He cut her off by shutting her door as he spoke. "Here's your tow now." He waved a red truck with a big crane contraption on the back to drive around her. The truck pulled into the space in front of Cam.

She spoke to the door as Officer Snippy shut it. "Maybe this mechanic dude can figure it out quickly and get Cam started." In a perfect world, she could then drive into the garage and not be too awfully late.

Who was she kidding? She didn't live in a perfect world. There was no such thing.

The officer walked to the front and met the short, stocky man in blue coveralls. At least this guy was wearing a smile. Of course, he was. He was about to make some cash—her cash—which she hadn't planned for. The men spoke briefly, and the officer returned to her door.

She cracked it a hair, and he leaned toward the opening. "Pop the lid."

She did, and the mechanic lifted Cam's hood.

A couple seconds later, the cop leaned down again. "Give her a try now."

Nothing.

Officer Ayers instructed. "Try again."

She did. Cam still refused to start.

The policeman shook his head and carefully opened her door. "Get out. Stay close to the car. I'll walk beside you, so you're safe."

Hope drained from her head, bypassing her heart, and oozed out her chest. Just want she needed. Tall and Cranky was urgently waiting, so she snatched her purse, grabbing the phone from it, and holding it in hand allowed the disgruntled policeman to assist her out and to the front.

He waved to indicate the stocky man closing Cam's hood. "This is Carl Carter. He's going to tow your vehicle to his lot."

The shorter man glanced at his hand, he'd wiped with a rag pulled from his hip pocket, then extended it to her. "Nice to meet you, ma'am." Carl flipped her a business card pulled from another pocket. "Here you go. Call later to find out the diagnosis."

She swallowed a lump in her throat and shook the car doctor's hand, holding back tears. "Thanks, Mr. Carter. Please, don't work on Cam without consulting me first."

"No ma'am."

She glanced at her ride. "I don't know what to do. Everything I own is in that car."

Sad but true. She studied Cam as though she might offer a solution. *Pathetic.* Everything she cared about fit into the trunk and back seat of a medium-sized sedan.

Embarrassing too. What did the good-looking, high-strung police officer think of her? He'd already shown her what he thought. She was inept, irresponsible, a little wacky and now homeless. He was almost right.

Carl sounded confident, "We'll take care of your possessions, miss. No worries."

She gave the mechanic her phone number. "Bree Collins."

Ayers butted in, "Your things will be safe with Mr. Carter."

"Yes, ma'am, Miss Collins. I'll lock her up tight as a preacher's wallet at a benefit."

"Okay, I'll call you later."

For the bad news. How was she going to afford repairs?

The policeman appeared content to watch the flow of cars passing by as the mechanic snapped a big hook to the underbelly of Cam's front end.

She put her phone to her ear and hit send on the contact marked Mya Landry. A familiar voice came on the phone. "Hi, darling, how far are you?"

"Actually, I'm out front of the mall. My car died, and I'm blocking the street."

"I'll call you a tow truck," Aunt Mya offered.

"It's okay. A policeman arrived, and he called a wrecker. They're getting ready to tow the car. Oops, they're done. Got to go."

"Okay, darling. I'll walk out to meet you." Mya clicked off, and Bree plopped the phone into her bag hanging from her shoulder.

"We're good to go." Carl stuck a clipboard with a form on it and pointed to a line. "Sign here." She did, and he pulled a sheet out and handed it to her. She folded the yellow paper and stuck it in her purse.

Carl walked to the driver's side of the wrecker and climbed in. The officer put his hand to Bree's back, indicating they should walk to the front. He guided her to the front, his broad mitt scorching her back. Once at the curb, the tow truck driver waved. With a few clangs of metal, Carl drove taking everything Bree owned. Her heart went with them.

She turned, shoulders sagging. "There's my aunt now."

The fashionista of the family trotted toward her on stilettos so high she appeared to totter, but elegantly. The woman waved and panted to a stop beside them, looking like she'd stepped off a Paris runway.

Slim hips draped with a fine, linen, summer skirt suit. The jacket's thin collar was open wide across the top, showing a pale shoulder and closed along one side with fabric covered buttons. The form-fitting top ended at a tiny waist. Icy blue color matched the glow of her eyes. Pumps were of the most delicate, flesh-toned leather. Aunt Mya probably paid more for the outfit than Bree had ever made in a month's time.

Mya Landry threw arms around her niece. Bree's troubles melted from stone-hard to somewhere between molten lava and Jell-O® texture. Being in a new place had seemed like an adventure when Aunt Mya offered her the job.

Cam's situation had turned Bree's adventure into a nightmare. Was the car as nervous as Bree? Silly girl, she's just a machine. Was it even possible her trusted ride had soaked up some of Bree's apprehension about her escapade turning into a possible disaster?

Aunt Mya was an oasis of calm. Bree was grateful for her aunt's touch, hoping she could absorb some of the older woman's much-needed confidence. Her own had withered along the roadway on the long trip.

Mya pushed her away and looked her in the eye. "I'm so happy you're finally here, Bree. You're going to be a God send. I just know it. This was meant to be." Mya stood a few inches shorter than Bree's five-foot-four inches, but her mini stature did nothing to detract from her self-assurance and poise.

She showed Mya the business card Carl had given her. "I'm happy to finally be here too. Sorry to arrive with a walloping bang. Cam was towed to this place." It was only a little, white lie. If she told it to Mya, maybe Bree would believe it herself. She could only hope.

Mya slipped an arm around Bree's waist. "You're in good hands, Bree. Carl Carter is the best mechanic in the area, and his shop isn't far from here."

Bree glanced down at her feet. "All my stuff is in the car." She winced. "Holy crap, I forgot to grab my heels."

She had worn her best pants suit for the trip, hoping to fit in, but she had no idea what type of environment she was heading for. Aunt Mya had referred to her business as, "a little lady's store in a mall." Bree had expected a small shop in a little strip mall.

Nothing had prepared her for what she was facing. This was anything but. It was the most elegant plaza she'd ever seen. There was nothing in Hazard to compare to this place, with its fancy restaurants and world-renowned brand stores, the likes of which she'd never expected to see, much less shop in. Hell, they didn't sell these labels at the finest store in her hometown.

And here she was, wearing her best pair of running shoes. Way to fit in, Bree. She'd laid her pumps on the floorboard of the passenger seat, where they remained, opting for comfort of driving in flats.

Aunt Mya snickered in a ladylike fashion, tapping a finger to her nose. "No problem, Bree. We'll fix that when we get to my office."

Chief Ayers glanced down at her feet then back at her, replacing the grin on his chiseled face with a smile. "Carl will make sure your possessions are safe." Officer Snippy said in a much calmer tone than before. Fine wrinkles around his gorgeous gray eyes had eased to smooth.

Mya beamed up at the tall, attractive police officer. "I see you're in good hands with Chief Ayers. He and I are old friends. Good to see you, Rex."

Chief Ayers gave her what looked like a genuine, warmhearted smile. "Mya, you're looking lovely, as always."

Mya didn't bother with a blush. "You're sweet to say so. A woman never tires of being told how good she looks. Speaking of which, this is my beautiful niece." She cocked her head toward Bree. "Did you take your maiden-name back after that nasty divorce, dear?"

Well, that was quick. Get the fact Bree was a throwaway bride out of the way. "No, it was too much trouble to switch. I've earned the name Collins. Wouldn't you say?"

Mya studied her expression, as though trying to read her mood. "You sure went through enough with that man. You're better off without the cheating windbag."

Bree's face burned to red. Here we go. Not only was she a loser divorcee. She'd been tossed aside for a slutty employee. Did Chief Ayers need to know her bra size too? "Yes, Aunt Mya, I completely agree. I'm sure Chief Ayers has better things to do than stand here and listen to us rehash my tainted history."

Mya ran a hand up her forearm. "I'm sorry, Bree. I didn't mean to embarrass you."

How red was her face, anyway? She wasn't angry with Mya. Knowing her as well as she did, her aunt was attempting to set her up with the good-looking officer. Misguided as her efforts were, it warmed Bree's heart. Mya wanted all good things for her. She was the closest thing Bree had to a mother now, and the only living relative Bree was aware of.

Ayers shuffled his feet and glanced away. "I need to move my cruiser and check in with the station. See you ladies later. Miss Collins, it's nice to meet you." He tipped his hat and sped toward his car.

He sure hadn't acted like it was nice, at least not at first. To be fair, she was putting a giant-sized crimp in his day by blocking rush hour traffic. Her attitude under duress couldn't have helped the situation, so maybe she was partly to blame for their rough beginning.

Mya turned toward the entrance and started walking. "Let's go. I want to show you around and introduce you to the staff."

Bree did her best to keep up with her aunt's quick stride. How could someone so small, wearing such high heels, move so fast?

"Is Chief Ayers really a friend of yours, or were you just being nice?" As a business owner, it paid to stay on the good side of public officials. Should she give the dashing Chief Ayers benefit of the doubt?

Mya gushed. "Oh, absolutely. Rex's wife worked for me ten years ago, when I opened the shop. He's a dear friend."

*Wonderful. S*he had alienated her aunt's friend.

Rex Ayres was married. How did a woman put up with him?

Fresh Starts, Dirty Money

CHAPTER TWO

Ayers pulled his ride into the parking lot at the
precinct and peeled his long frame from the car.
Stretching he mused at how adorable the irate female
had looked, obviously curbing her desire to scream
obscenities to him. It wasn't that he took joy in
annoying a woman, and to be fair, she'd had every
right to be angry. To her credit, she'd controlled what
looked like a spicy temper. That's what had piqued
his interest, then made him feel exposed, and
compounded into his bad behavior.

He had no right to pass his bad mood on to
pedestrians. Yeah, he'd had to face life and death,
mostly death, before meeting the perplexed but
charming female with the bouncy, ginger curls
stopping just short enough to show off her long, sleek
neck. It didn't give him the right to be a grumpy, old

grizzly clawing at the first living being he encountered after the disaster that had been his morning. It was his job to ensure safety of the public, not to incite or torment them.

He'd poked a good one with the little cutie in that broken down Toyota sedan. Sure, it had stopped smack-dab in the middle of rush hour traffic, blocking a main fairway leading to the bridge over the Ohio River, but he shouldn't have insinuated she had failed to maintain a proper vehicle. A number of issues could cause an electrical malfunction.

The worst part was who the gal had turned out to be. Mya had gone on and on for as long as they'd been friends, talking about her delightful niece. She'd been overjoyed learning the woman had finally taken her offer for a job and planned to move to Northern Kentucky to work for her.

Way to go, Dickhead.

He'd made an ass of himself, probably ruined his chance to befriend the newcomer. Mya would never forgive him for treating her precious niece that way. He'd probably ruined a valuable friendship. Mya would never forgive him for treating her precious niece that way. No doubt, the gal would elaborate about his rude treatment.

He snickered to himself as he entered the bullpen. The cute little lady had referred to her Camry as Cam. Several officers were milling about, some working at their desks. He made his way to the coffee stand and poured himself a cup.

Officer Van Carter strolled over for a refill. "What's tickled your giggle bone, Chief?"

Ayers took a sip and huffed out a breath. "It's been a hell of a morning, but something stuck me funny."

"Like what?" Van tilted his head quizzically.

Ayers spoke loud enough for officers in the bullpen to hear, "Carter, do you call your vehicle by name?"

Van smiled. "Sure, it's Ram, for Ram Charger."

"What about you, Martin? You name your ride?" He turned toward the bullpen.

Officer Rusty Martin looked up from his computer, the most muscular dude on the force. "Oh yeah. Of course. I call my pickup Stud. He can handle anything I throw at him."

Ayers laughed. "What about you, Izzy?"

Izzy Comings, the only female police officer in the room laughed. "Why are you asking?" She studied him with a critical glare.

"No biggie. Just wondering how many people named their cars. I ran up on a driver today who called her car Cam. I thought it was funny. That's all."

"Nothing funny about it, and yeah. I call her Sally."

The chief sat his cup down. "Seriously? That's a girl's name."

Izzy stood her five-foot-four, legs apart, and thumbs in her utility belt. "Mustang Sally, that is."

They all laughed. Ayers conceded his err in judgement. "Guess it's not so strange after all." He strolled into his office with his cup. The others went back to work. His thoughts remained on the spunky female whose face pinked from irritation. The one who walked away from her precious automobile while it carried away her every possession. Who had moved to an unfamiliar location to start a new career. In a place where she only knew one living soul, and who he had made fun of and poked like a bear in a cage. He was more than pitiful.

Hopefully, he would get the opportunity to make amends and get to know the intriguing female with the slim hips and perky bust? The one whose silky curls caught the morning sunlight and shone like they were coated with gold flakes, making his fingers itch to touch them and tangle themselves in that mass of spirals?

Probably not. He'd blown it.

CHAPTER THREE

Aunt Mya led Bree through a quick tour of the fabulous mall shops, then to her pride and joy. Finally, they stood outside the entrance to the store. Mya splayed a hand wave as though showing it off.

Giant black and gold italic print in an elegant style read 'Pampered Tigress' on the logo above a lengthy wall stylishly displaying a variety of departments inside where any woman could find her dream products.

"This is my little women's shop." None of those adjectives did service to the massive, elaborate set up. "I built Pampered Tigress around the theme of giving the discerning woman everything she could want in the way of pampering under one roof. Behind the small sitting area as we enter the store is the fragrance department. To the left is the skin care and makeup department, where one can shop or make an appointment for a facial or makeover. We sell our select, exclusive brand of cosmetics and skin care, perfected by yours truly. Past that is the hair salon and day spa, where a lady can treat herself to every possible form of relaxation from any type of massage desired, to body wraps, reiki, cupping, or candling. From the entry to the right is the hat, purse, and scarf department; and past that is the shoe salon. We carry only the exclusive, highest quality brands. Some I designed myself."

"Wow, she's really something. I had no idea your 'little shop' was so fabulous or that you were multi-talented." Bree expelled a whiff, feeling even more ridiculous without her heels, even if they were off the rack department store bought, like her clothing. "You have everything here except for clothing."

"Yes, indeed. The surrounding retailers handle that very well." Mya's hand swept behind her to stores branding Neiman Marcus®, Louis Vuitton®, Versace®, Chanel®, Christian Dior®. The only thing missing seemed to be bridal, but that wasn't something a woman needed every day.

Mya beamed. "I'm thrilled you decided to take me up on my offer. I've spent the last ten years working my buns off putting this store together. It's my baby. I never had time for travel, adventure, marriage, or a family of my own. You've been at odds with what to do with that new MBA of yours. I thought, what better way to use it? I need help, someone I can train to co-manage the store with me. Take some of the burden off my shoulders, so I can make time for other things in life."

"Like men and marriage?" Bree studied her aunt's face.

"Men, for sure. Marriage, maybe, but not likely. I'm too old and set in my ways to live with a man. That doesn't mean I don't want to spend time with one." Mya winked conspiratorially.

Bree gave her best interrogation glance at Mya. "Anyone in particular?"

"Well, it just so happens, I do have a fella. We've been seeing each other regularly for about three months, and it's been rough finding the time. I want more of that."

Curious, Bree hadn't heard of this man who had peeked her aunt's interest. "Tell me about this fella of yours." She followed her aunt though the elegant store to a back wall, through double doors and down a short hallway to an office sectioned off by a glass panel. As they walked, their conversation continued.

"His name is James Franks, and he's the developer who built my subdivision. He lives in the house across the street from me, built originally as the model home. He's extremely handsome, worldly, brilliant, and charming. He's very busy himself, so he doesn't complain about me devoting so much time to my business; but I'd like to spend more time with him."

"Well, I hope to get up to speed quickly, so you can do just that. I can hardly express how much I appreciate you inviting me to come, offering me a job and a place to stay. I won't disappoint you, and I'll find a home of my own soon as possible."

She vowed to herself not to overstay her welcome. Aunt Mya meant too much to her, and she didn't want to take advantage of her generosity more than necessary.

"Nonsense. I live in a big, rambling house. It's lonely. I'd adore having you stay permanently…if you want. You're the closest I have to a daughter of my own. Now your mother has passed away, God rest her soul, you are my only family."

Bree had been lost after her mom died a few months back. "And you mine, Aunt Mya. I can't believe how generous you're being. I'm overwhelmed." The woman was too good to her. Bree blinked back tears trying to force their way out.

Mya shrugged. "Just keep it in mind for now, Dear. Nothing is written in stone. There's one thing. I'd like you to call me Mya at the store. I believe it will help my staff accept you quicker and respect your authority if you don't refer to me as Aunt Mya. It's not a secret. It just sounds more professional."

Bree nodded. "I understand. No problem." She followed Mya through a set of glass doors into an office area.

A tall, thin blonde woman about Bree's age, with short-cropped hair stood behind a sleek, white, enamel desk. The office was ultra-modern, all black and white—mostly white. A large modern-art painting of something barely resembling a black and red rose hung on the wall behind the woman's desk.

The stunning female could've been a fashion model with her slim figure and nearly six-foot tall stature. Dressed like one in a streamlined, linen, sheath dress of the softest green, her matching eyes sparkled as she greeted her boss with a smile.

Mya beamed at Bree then the tall gal. "Bree, this is my assistant, Kaylee Armstrong. Kaylee, this is Bree Collins, my niece, and our new store Assistant Manager. Bree is going to be learning the ropes by working a week in each department."

Bree stuck a hand toward the blonde. "Good to meet you, Kaylee."

Kaylee shook her hand firmly. "Likewise, and welcome, Bree." Bree could tell instantly she was going to like the pleasant woman.

Mya waved a hand toward doorway beside the one with her name on it. "That will be your office, Bree."

Bree's heart did a tap dance at the gold lettering on the wall plate reading 'Bree Collins, Asst. Manager.'

Mya must've noticed the jump in her niece's heartrate. "Kaylee is getting your computer and phone lines set up, and she will assist you with anything you need. She doesn't keep our calendars or type memos. That's easier for us to handle. She manages company reports, salaries, timesheets, paychecks, expense accounts, and special business projects."

"My, you have a lot on your place, Kaylee. I'll try not to be a burden." Bree had never had a personal assistant before, even a shared one. At the law firm, she'd been the one who had provided the assistance. This was going to take getting used to.

Kaylee met Bree's eyes. "We'll be fine. No worries. Your connections will be finished this afternoon. The tech guy should be here later today to work on them."

Bree was itching to open her door and inspect her own office. This one had a door. She'd never had a door before. "Thank you, Kaylee."

Mya entered her personal realm. Despite the urge to inspect her own cubicle, Bree followed her inside and shut the door. "Let's get you outfitted with some heels. You're a size seven. Right?"

She opened a closet behind her huge glass topped desk. The wall behind her was covered with drawers and doors of various sizes.

"Yeah, thanks." Bree glanced around her.

The black and white theme continued in Mya's office, with her walls adorned by two matching modern-art paintings of red roses along the longest wall. The direction opposite Mya's desk area held a round, glass table with four cushy-looking, black, leather chairs. Behind that along a wall a white, leather couch looked so soft a person could lose oneself in its cushions.

Mya sat a pair of black Jimmy Choo's in front of her. "These should work, and they'll compliment your outfit. You look nice, Bree."

The praise was special, coming from Mya. She didn't sugar coat things. If she said Bree looked good, she did. Bree picked the pumps up.

Red soles weren't yet marred from use, and insoles showed little wear. Bree slid her foot inside the soft, red, leather heels. A sensation of sophistication swam up her legs and filled her with an instant boost of confidence. *Who said a good pair of shoes couldn't make the woman?* Her shoulders lifted, and her neck straightened. She'd never worn anything so decadently lovely, and her bland, black pantsuit suddenly took on a fresh shine.

"Wow, Mya, these are amazing. They're barely worn. Are you sure you want to loan them to me for the day? What if I scuff them? It would take a week's salary to replace them." She could go buy herself another pair of heels, but not in this mall. Her budget wasn't up to it.

Mya waved a hand. "Certainly, Bree. Shoes are meant to be worn. Possessions aren't worth having if you can't enjoy them. Wear the heels. Keep them long as you want. I keep a handy stash here. You never know when you might break a heel. Sometimes I like to change before going out for the evening."

Her feet did not want to come out of these shoes. Who was Bree to argue? "Okay, if you say so. Thank you."

They spent the good part of the day meeting staff, learning the lay of the land, and going over reports. Mya gave her a rundown of what she expected during training, then what she would expect once Bree was officially her Assistant Manager.

Bree could hardly contain her enthusiasm. This was a dream job, and her new life a fantasy come true.

CHAPTER FOUR

Aunt Mya carried the last carton inside and sat it at the foot of the steps for Bree to take to her room. "What did Carl say was wrong with your car?"

"He found a corroded electrical connection in the ignition module. After checking the switch, he cleaned the oxidized terminals and replaced wires. Cam is good as new. That snotty cop implied I had failed to take good care of her. Cam has seen me through college, lean years when I put Owen through law school, and while he was getting his law firm up and running. She's like an old friend, and I take good care of her. I resent his implying otherwise." Bree picked up the tote and started up the stairs.

"You really should give Rex a break. He's an amazing guy. I've never known him to be rude or condescending with anyone. Sure, he's a cop and all. There must be instances when he is required to be tough, but your car breaking down isn't one of those situations. I'm sure he was just having a bad day." Mya stood at the foot of the stairs with hands on hips.

Bree might be a bit sensitive when it came to Cam. She had been nervous as hell when she arrived, not used to such traffic, and tired from the long trip. Her beloved sedan had been the one thing she could count on over the last years, and he'd all but laughed at her. "You could be right. I'll be nice to Chief Ayers for your sake. I won't embarrass you with your old friend, but don't expect us to become chummy."

Mya leaned on the handrail. "Good. Rex is a special man; and he's had it rough."

Bree hadn't given Ayers' personal life much consideration. She'd been wrapped up in her own fit of anxiety. "If you say so. Hey, does his wife still come in? Kaylee said she was nice, and that you and she had a special bond."

Mya's smile dropped, and her voice lowered softly. "Yes, and I miss her terribly. She was with me for seven years…until she took ill. Cancer. It took her swiftly. Within three months she was gone."

Bree sat the box down and put her arms around her aunt. "I'm sorry, Aunt Mya. I didn't know. That was insensitive of me."

So, the striking but brisk Police Chief was a widower. It had been years since his wife passed, so that wasn't an excuse for bad behavior. Her feathers were still bristled from their rough start. Time for a change of subject.

Bree looked toward the picture window in the front of the house. "What's with the burnout on the corner?"

Mya frowned and sat on the steps. "Oh, that's Ms. Barnes' house. She's about eighty and lived alone, bought the house right before I got this one and moved in. Lucky for her, it's next door to Jimmy's home." It was cute the way Aunt Mya referred to her fella, James Franks, as Jimmy.

Bree put her box down, sat beside her, and took her hand. "Boy, it seems I have a habit of bringing up sad subjects."

Mya patted her hand and smiled. "It's okay, Bree. It turned out fine, except for Ms. Barnes' house is a goner."

Bree squeezed her palm. "You want to talk about it?"

"Of course." Mya smiled sweetly. "Jimmy and I came home around ten that night, and I was getting ready for bed when I heard sirens. I ran outside, and the street was filled with emergency vehicles. Two police cruisers, two fire trucks, an ambulance, and several media vans were circling her house. Jimmy ran out of the burning house with his arms around Ms. Barnes, both with towels over their head. He helped her over to where I met them at the end of my driveway. Police officers were keeping onlookers and media at bay, but they kept clambering to get interviews and photos of Jimmy and Ms. Barnes."

Bree recalled many times helping Oran's clients elude the press before or after trials. "They can be persistent and downright offensive."

"Indeed, they can." Mya smiled. "Anyway, Ms. Barnes was a basket case and not in the mood for interviews. Neither was Jimmy. That house went up in flames quickly after they escaped. You can see what little was left of it, when the Fire Department finished putting out the blaze. Jimmy didn't want a big deal made of it. Still yet, they managed to use a zoom lens or something to get a couple shots, one of them running from the burning house and one on my doorstep. The story made front page news the next day." She stood and opened a foyer table drawer, turned, and handed a clipping to Bree. "Here's the article. I keep it tucked away because Jimmy acts embarrassed by all the attention."

Bree took the paper and perused it. A grainy photograph of two people fleeing a burning ranch-style home was in the top right corner. Center page above the fold held a larger, more crisp shot of Aunt Mya with an arm around an elderly woman in a floral nightgown. A grey-haired, handsome man stood beside them his face turned toward activity of the first responders. He appeared unaware his photo was being taken.

She handed the paper back to Mya. "Your Jimmy is as handsome as you said, Aunt Mya. Why's was he so upset about having his photo taken. The man is clearly a hero."

Mya folded it and stashed it away in the drawer. "You're right, Bree. He is, but Jimmy is very shy."

That didn't make sense. "But he's a big deal builder and developer. Surely, he's used to being in the limelight."

Mya shook her head. "Oh, he's not timid about publicizing his work; but he prefers attention on his property, not on him personally."

Impressive, a successful man who didn't want to draw attention to himself—nothing like her braggart ex-husband. Oran Collins took every chance to get his photo in the papers, except when Bree showed him the ammunition, she used to get a decent divorce settlement. "How did Jimmy come to save Ms. Barnes?"

Mya wore a grim face and leaned against the banister. "He went into his home office after we returned home, to pay some bills for his next venture, the subdivision he's starting. He bought a large tract of land a couple blocks away where this one ends for another phase of homebuilding. He's just waiting on some permits to break ground on it. Anyway, he opened the back French doors for fresh air and smelled smoke. When he stepped out back, he could see curtains burning in Ms. Barnes' dining room. He called 911 and grabbed the first tool he could find in his shed—a golf club—then ran next door. Pounding on her front door got no answer. Neither did thumping on her kitchen door. He whacked a pane in the French doors with the club and unlocked them. Jimmy reached in and let himself inside. He kept calling, but she didn't answer. The house was filled with thick smoke, so he kept his head down and made his way into the front of the house to the hallway and her bedroom. Her door was open, and she was asleep. Smoke was starting to fill the bedroom by then, and flames were spreading into the living room and kitchen. He couldn't wake her, so he grabbed a couple of towels from her bathroom, wet them then and placed one over her head and one over his. He carried her out the front door to safety, as help arrived. By the time he got her to my driveway, she was coming to. She'd been dead from smoke inhalation if he hadn't gotten to her in time. EMTs gave her oxygen and insisted Jimmy take some too."

From the looks of the shambles left of her home, Mrs. Barnes would've likely been burned to a crisp without waking, had he not rescued her. "That poor woman. Where is she now? What will happen to her?" Bree had been focusing on her own problems, whining about all that had gone helter-skelter in her life. At least she had a lovely place to live, a fabulous job, the opportunity for a fresh start, and she was young enough to make one at the age of thirty. Poor, elderly Ms. Barnes had lost everything she owned, burned to a cinders.

Bree vowed to start focusing on the positive. Negativity got enough attention. She didn't want to draw more of it to herself.

Mya smiled easily. "She called her sister in a nearby town. She told Ms. Barnes to come live with her. She didn't have anything to move but said she had good insurance and would call them the next day. The Fire Marshal asked how she wanted to manage cleanup. She told him her insurance would cover the cost, so the city could remove rubble and bill her. They're supposed to handle that later this week. Anyway, once EMTs dubbed her well enough, Rex had one of his police officers drive her to the sister's house. I haven't seen her since, but it was only last week."

Curiosity grew by the minute, about the intriguing guy who had won her independent aunt's heart. "Your Jimmy sounds like quite a man." After all these years as a single woman, it was a surprise to find Aunt Mya falling in love; and from what Bree gathered, for the first time.

Mya glowed. "He sure is. I feel like a twenty-year-old around him. I haven't been this giddy over a man since I was in college. Jimmy is dashing, sophisticated, worldly, intelligent, and treats me like a queen."

Bree stood. "You deserve to be treated like that. Mom said the two of you had a blast while you were in college together. From what I understand, the 1970s university scene was wild. I can see the two of you with long hair; hip-hugger, bell-bottom jeans; and tube tops bopping from frat party to frat party."

Mya chuckled. "Not to mention protests and sit-ins. It was a time of war and demonstrations, fighting against 'the system.' Now here I am, a professional."

Bree retrieved her last bin of possessions. "Funny, we live and learn. It is an ever-changing world. If we don't shift with it, we get buried by the stampede forward. I can't wait to meet your Jimmy."

As Bree climbed the steps with her load, her aunt's voice trailed behind her. "We have a dinner meeting tomorrow evening with the city council. I'll ask him which night he has free, and we can have him over to dinner."

"Great, I love to cook. I haven't done much of it since Mom died. Cooking for one is no fun." With Oran out of the house, she'd survived on cheese and crackers, bagels, yogurt, cereal, and canned soups since her mother had passed away.

Bree carried her burden into her bright, sunny bedroom. A wave of gratitude washed over her. She was a lucky gal, to have Mya in her life.

Mya stood in the doorway. "We'll see. It depends on how busy we are at the shop. Most times I just call an order in and pick it up at a restaurant on the way home. Jimmy understands. He'll be fine with whatever we serve. I'm excited for you to meet him."

James Franks seemed an enigma. Bree could hardly wait to check him out herself.

CHAPTER FIVE

After a cup of coffee at six with Mya, Bree left the house wearing shorts, sports bra, and favorite running shoes. She wanted to get a few miles in before heading to the courthouse to have her driver's license transferred and renewed. The DMV office opened at eight. Mya was heading to work so Bree would see her later at the shop.

Mya waved to the right. "Go right. Run two blocks to a quiet country lane that separates our subdivision, and the one Jimmy is going to develop as his next project. You'll see the signs. You can run up and down that road safely. It's a two-lane road, rarely used and only by people who know the area well." Bree could run, grab a shower, freshen up, and meet Mya at Pampered Tigress after completing her errand.

Early morning air was crisp and cool. Dew was starting to burn off as the sun rose. She was getting into the groove of her stride when she turned left onto the small roadway. To her left was the subdivision. To her right was a patch of thick woods that opened about fifty yards ahead to a vast clearing. The sidewalk was only on the subdivision side of the road, which hadn't been paved for many years. Lines on blacktop had dulled and worn away from traffic and weather.

As she approached the clearing, a muddy drive used for traffic onto the land under development came into view. Gravel had yet to be poured to form an easy entrance. The once muddy ground had been compacted by vehicles and hardened into ruts.

Seven huge pieces of construction equipment, one with a thick roller in front and one with a tall crane, its hook suspended high above the orange contraption, squatted at the road entrance. A wooden sign held several pieces of paper beneath a thick plastic sash, announcing it as the site of the Franks Development.

After running a mile along the road, and another back, the machinery remained the only sign of activity. James Franks' property looked eerily bizarre sitting idle, waiting for someone to put the expensive machinery to use.

Behind the glass walled countertop at the courthouse, the pretty brunette's badge identified her as Candy Palmer, County Clerk. "Welcome to Campbell County, Bree Collins." Candy took the driver's license, and a slip of paper Bree handed her with Mya's address on it. "I'll be just a minute."

"No problem." Bree smiled and picked up a brochure from the countertop to peruse while Candy went to a desk and typed in the changes on a machine.

Loud voices came from the back wall behind the bullpen where Candy worked. Two doors were closed, and a third along a side wall led out to the hallway for the workers' use. Bree had used a similar door on the visitor's side of the counter to enter the Clerk's office from the hallway. One of the back doors held a black and gold plaque reading 'Judge Executive,' and the other read 'Planning & Zoning Commissioner.' It was difficult to tell from behind which door the voices came, but it was clear the individuals inside were having a row.

A glance at Candy, showed her cheeks pinking with embarrassment. Her lips pursed, and she kept her face toward her typing. She stood and met Bree's amused gaze. Her eyes rolled upward with a minute shrug, then she motioned to the door. "Ms. Collins, I'll be just a minute. Your license is printing now. The machine is across the hall. I'll be right back."

"No worries." Bree smiled.

After the clerk left the office, the angry voices grew louder. She was able to make out bits and pieces of conversation, but not enough to hear the whole argument. There was something about, "money you've grown accustomed to," and, "you'll be sorry."

The door flung open. A well-dressed, silver-haired man appeared in the doorway facing the person inside. "I'll be here bright and early tomorrow. I expect those signed permits on your desk waiting for me. Or else!" He pounded a fist against the doorframe.

The enraged fella spun, and without facing Bree's side of the room, stormed out the hallway door, nearly bumping into Candy as she tried to enter. His face was red from the argument and flustered from nearly plowing the clerk down. He was handsome in a middle-aged sort of way, and she recognized him instantly from the photograph.

James Franks smiled, and his face softened with a slight nod of the head. "Oh, Ms. Palmer, please excuse me. I'm so sorry." Anger drained from his face, and he went from irate to charming in an instant.

Candy bypassed him. "Not a problem, Mr. Franks." As the door shut behind her, she rolled her eyes and shook her head, more to herself than for Bree's benefit.

Jimmy? Bree's heart tightened in her chest.

Stepping to the counter, Candy laid Bree's new license on the countertop. "Sorry about that, Ms. Collins. Those two butt heads all the time. Can't seem to get along, but they have to work together."

"Oh? Why is that?" Bree couldn't resist trying to pull more out of Candy.

The clerk didn't act opposed to a bit of gossip. "Well, Mr. Franks is developing a new neighborhood here in town. Mr. Rose, Jefferson Rose, is the Planning & Zoning Coordinator in charge of getting the ordinances cleared with the P&Z Committee and administering proper, legal, documentation allowing the expansion."

Bree put pieces of the puzzle together. "So, permits? Is there an issue? Those guys were pretty heated."

Candy seemed to ponder the question then shook her head. "I don't believe so. Nothing special I've heard. Sometimes paperwork takes time. You know, attorneys and all."

Boy did she. Her slithering snake of a husband had soured her taste for lawyers.

Candy pushed an invoice her way. "All righty then. That will be twenty-two dollars."

Bree shoved the bills to Candy and pocketed the invoice, unconvinced it was nothing special. There was more to their rift than merely not getting along; and it wasn't just tension from normal paper-pushing. From what she'd heard, their argument alluded to a possible payoff or grafting of cash for permit compliance.

Was Jefferson Rose getting a kickback from the developer or a payoff to force through permits out of compliance? Could Jimmy be using inferior material or something of that nature? Whatever it was, they were up to something not quite legal. James had clearly threatened the Planning & Zoning Commissioner. That was certain .

Aunt Mya was right. James Franks had flipped on the charm the instant he came in contact with Candy Palmer. His actions reeked of womanizer, or at least of manipulator. What had Mya gotten involved in with this guy?

Distrust swelled in her gut. Bree's protective nature jumped into gear. Was James Franks anything like the man Aunt Mya believed him to be? She was going to find out. Jimmy was not going to hurt Mya—not like Oran had hurt Bree.

Later, over lunch and spreadsheets in Mya's office, Bree decided to bring it up. "I believe I saw your fella, James Franks, at the courthouse today. He was leaving the P&Z office."

Mya smiled brightly. "Oh, what did you think of Jimmy? I wish I'd been there."

Bree sat her chicken salad sandwich down. "We didn't exactly meet. He was leaving, and I was in the County Clerk's office. He didn't see me; but she said he was Mr. Franks, the developer. I figured it had to be your Jimmy."

Mya gave her a conspiratorial wink. "Handsome, isn't he? Well, you'll meet soon enough."

"Dashing," Bree couldn't disagree. "He and the commissioner were having a loud, heated argument. Candy said they always butt heads."

Mia waved a hand down dismissively. "Oh, business of course. It was probably just a misunderstanding. You know how men are. Jimmy is passionate about his work. He has been under stress waiting for his. I believe they've been delayed, and it's costing him money. I don't interfere with his work, and he doesn't stick his nose into mine. You understand."

Bree silently nodded, thinking about the idle equipment sitting on James Franks' vacant property.

No, but I'm going to learn.

CHAPTER SIX

Bree stood quietly observing in a corner of the small meeting room as her aunt interrogated a teenaged shoplifter. Albert Bane's five-foot-six, or so, middle-aged, uniformed frame propped against the far wall, arms crossed above his pudgy belly.

The girl looked to be about seventeen at the most, wearing pricy clothing, a stylish cropped hairdo, and her makeup done beautifully. A loose overshirt buttoned up the front. A tee shirt beneath that tucked into her slim fitting jeans. It wasn't unusual for an affluent girl her age to shop in the store. She didn't appear to be a needy girl. So, why was she shoplifting?

Mya sat patiently with hands clasped on the table between them. "You were caught red handed with a bottle of three-hundred-dollar perfume, a fifty-dollar compact, a three-hundred-fifty-dollar pair of gloves, and a silk scarf with a four-hundred-dollar price tag. That's a thousand dollars' worth of merchandise, all neatly tucked inside your under-shirt. What do you have to say for yourself?"

The girl shrugged, wringing her hands together on the tabletop. She had managed to slip stolen items down her perky cleavage, to carry them against her flat tummy above the waistline. Clever kid, but not clever enough to escape keen eyes of Albert Bane, store Security Guard.

Albert had spotted her on one of his many screens. She had bent forward to spray perfume on her neck. When she turned away, the bottle was missing from the counter. Upon arrest, they'd found she had alluded Albert's watchful eye in other departments before he finally caught her.

Mya sat back in her chair. "Okay, dear. Mr. Bane has contacted the police. You're going to jail for this." She stood as the girl expelled a huff of air. Mya hesitated a second, but when the girl refused to talk, she turned and left the room. Mya and Mr. Bane followed her into the hallway.

Chief Rex Ayers entered the office suite from the hallway. He stuck a hand toward Mya who shook it. "Mya, I understand from Bane, you've nabbed yourselves a shoplifter." Then he shoved it to Bane. "Good job, Albert."

Mya took control of the situation. "Yes, thank you for coming Chief. Mr. Bane, you can go back to your station. I'm sure Chief Ayers can handle this from here." Bane left them with a nod and headed to his office observatory station. "Chief, you remember my niece, Bree Collins, don't you?

Rex Ayer's cheeks pinked slightly, and he grimaced. "Of course, she is difficult to forget. Good to see you again, Ms. Collins." The hand shoved toward Bree.

She hesitated momentarily and then placed hers inside his. The big mitt dwarfed her slim hand, but she gave it a hearty, businesslike shake, trying her best to ignore the sip of electricity that sizzled into her palm and up her arm at his touch. Did the man have an internal furnace that made all that heat, or was it in her head?

"Listen, Rex, now Bane is gone I want to talk with you. This girl attempted to steal a thousand dollars' worth of items. She had the merchandise on her body when Albert apprehended her. Did you find anything out about her, from the driver's license Kaylee faxed you?"

"I did. She's clean as a baby at a baptism. Not even a parking ticket. A thousand dollars puts this out of the misdemeanor category and into a Class D felony. A conviction comes with a mandatory prison sentence. How do you want to handle this?"

"Damn it. I was afraid you'd say that. Okay, I suspected as much. Here's what I want to do." "Take her to the station. Show her the photos. Explain to her that I'm not going to file charges…this time. If I ever get wind of her being arrested for any other crime—anything at all—I'll bring these photos to light and file a suit against her. She'll get more than the mandatory sentence for multiple violations. She's not welcome in my store any longer. Tell her we have input her face into our facial recognition program. She'll be arrested if she ever sets foot in the store again."

Rex's eyes went wide. "You have such a thing?" Facial recognition would have to be a costly security program, more than a store would be likely to afford.

Mya snickered. "Of course not, but she won't know that." He chuckled and let her finish. "Be sure to scare her straight."

"Will do, Mya. This is really big of you. Most would send her straight to lockup."

"I know," Mya groaned. "I can't see ruining that child's life without giving her a chance to straighten up and fly right." Mya beamed. "Thank you, Rex, for handling this discreetly." She turned and went into her office.

He faced Bree. "Ms. Collins, could I have a word before you go."

Mya's door clicked shut. Kaylee was busy typing something into a computer on her desk. Rex put a hand forward, and Bree reluctantly slipped hers into it, allowing him to pull her farther down the hallway for privacy.

"Listen, we got off to a rough start yesterday. I'd like the chance to make it up to you. I'm not that grumpy Gus you met yesterday. I'd love for us to become friends. Would you allow me to take you to dinner tonight? Maybe we could get to know each other better."

"Gee, I don't know." She'd promised to give him the benefit of a doubt, not to go out with the good-looking guy.

He put his hand up to interrupt her refusal. "If nothing else, let's try to get along for Mya. She means the world to me, and it's clear the two of you are close."

"Listen; I'm not even sure what time I'll get off work."

He saw it for the lame excuse it was. "How about this? I'll call you later, and you can tell me what you decide."

"I guess so. That sounds reasonable." It gave her a chance to back off if she chose to, and it was easier to reject someone over the phone.

"Give me this chance to prove I'm not a total ass." When he smiled, tiny wrinkles formed around his pale grey eyes, illuminating them even more than his strong personality already did, and making him look even more handsome than she'd remembered. There was the tiniest cleft in his chin, and the square jaw gave him a masculine appearance.

He smelled fresh, and an unmistakable scent combination both raw and dignified, reminding her both of a woody trail and brilliant sunlight of a white-hot dessert. It lent him the image of a powerful man who transcends time and radiated that same heat insider her veins.

Damn.

If a fragrance could do that for Rex, she needed to take her work in that department of the store more seriously. She grinned and snickered. "When you put it that way, how can I resist. I mean really, it's rare to find a man that's not a total ass. Rex, you've swept me off my feet with all this sweet talk." She chuckled.

He winked and turned to stroll toward the conference room. "Yeah, I'm a real charmer."

"You mind if I go in with you while you talk with the girl? I wouldn't mind seeing how you handle her. I promise not to interfere. I'm learning the ropes here." She nodded toward the room where the shoplifter waited.

He chuckled and winked again. "Okay, but I'm not turning the male magnetism on for her. I'm working here. I need to be stern and in control."

She saluted as he opened the door for her. "Got it, Chief." She took her previous place against the wall.

Chief Ayers strutted to the table, sat down, and gave the girl a chance to speak on her behalf. When she didn't, he showed her a series of photo stills Albert had sent him, of items she hand lifted on her freebee excursion. "Well, Ms. Baker, it appears you had quite a shopping spree. You racked up a hefty total."

The female's voice was meek and low, though she continued to sit erect, head held high. An air of dignity showed she was unaccustomed to being in such a situation. "That's all I was doing…shopping." She was clearly wealthy and used to having whatever she wanted dropped in her lap. Probably figured Daddy's attorney would get her off without consequences.

He nodded slowly and intently. "I see. It's rare for a person to hide merchandise they are going to buy on their body. These photos show your intent was to walk out without paying for them. That's shoplifting, and it's a criminal offence. The fact you tallied up a total over a thousand dollars makes it a major offence." He paused putting emphasis on those last two words, and giving them time to sink in. "In fact, it's a Class D felony. Conviction carries a sentence of a minimum one and up to five years in prison. That's not a day spa. It's hard time in a state facility."

As Rex spoke, the girl's color drained completely away. She turned white as snowy mountains in winters back home. All fight appeared to go out of her. Shoulders slumped, and her chin dipped low. Her eyes glassed over. "I…I…I'll go to prison…for a little shoplifting? Felony? This can't be happening." She blinked several times, and her eyes shot toward the ceiling to the side.

Rex let her stew for sever minutes. Finally, he scooped the photographs into a pile, picked them up, and then stood. The table met halfway between his crotch and knees. "Stand up and turn around."

Why did Bree have to notice his crotch, bulging below his thick utility belt?

I mean, really? Get a grip, girl. Sure, it had been year since she'd been laid, but seriously? Not the time. Not the place. Most definitely, not the guy. Or maybe it was. *Who knows?*

Ms. Baker sniffed, drawing Bree out of her fantasy world, and did as she was told. Rex towered over her, as he stepped around and cuffed her hands behind her. She kept blinking away tears to no avail. They left ruddy streaks down her immaculately applied makeup.

Bree followed as he ushered his prisoner out of the room, past Kaylee's desk and through the doors to the store. He turned his head before the door shut behind him and shot Bree a wink, mouthing the word, "Later."

Bree knocked on Mya's door and turned the knob at the answering, "Come in."

Working at a small, white laptop on her desk, Mya turned toward her. "What's up? I take it Rex handled that well."

Bree walked toward her. "Mind if I sit a minute? I wanted to run something by you."

"Sure." Mya folded hands in her lap and pushed her seat back a tad.

Bree took one of two guest chairs across from her desk. "It's about Chief Ayers."

"Is everything okay, Bree?" Mya's head tilted.

"Oh, yeah, sure. He ah…he asked me out to dinner tonight."

Mya's face went into a broad smile. "Wonderful. I just know the two of you will get along perfectly."

Bree winced and glared. "Really? We haven't exactly seen eye-to-eye yet. Listen, I know he's a good friend of yours, so I'm willing to cut him some slack. He's definitely attractive…in a macho kind of way. So, you think I should go?"

splayed hands on her glass top table. "You didn't refuse, did you?"

Bree blinked, flustered. "Oh, no, not exactly. I wasn't sure what time we'd get out of here tonight and didn't know if you had anything planned for the evening." She swallowed hard. "He's going to call me later.

"Well, I think it's marvelous. You should accept. Besides, I have that council thing. I'm meeting Jimmy at the hotel where we're having the dinner meeting. You two young people go on. Take Rex up on his offer. Get to know the fellow. You're just going to love him. Go enjoy yourself."

Bree wrung her hands in her lap. "Well, if you're busy and you say so. I guess, I'll go. What harm could it do? It's just dinner." It had been over two years since she'd been to dinner with a man, and that had been Orin. He had spent most of it taking calls with clients on his cellphone. Dinner with the good-looking police chief might be a worthy excursion.

"Great. Tell him to pick you up at six-thirty. Stop into my office around six. We need a few minutes before you go." Bree got up to go but stopped at her aunt's voice. "Bree, dear, pick a lovely fragrance from the store…something you will enjoy wearing over and over. Take a bottle for yourself…on the store."

"Wow, thanks, Aunt Mia." Any bottle she chose would cost more than she had made in a day at her old jobs. *What a treat.* She would have to find some way to pay her aunt back for her incredible generosity.

CHAPTER SEVEN

Bree got a massage and a facial during her lunch break and knocked on her aunt's office door at promptly six. "Come in, dear," came from behind the door. Mya stood, and Bree pranced toward her desk, giving her a demure smile. Mya chortled and put her hands on Bree's shoulders. "Someone had a makeover."

"Yes, and Charlotte is fabulous. She gave me a facial and did my makeup then bagged the products she used and handed them to me. She said you'd told her to."

"Yes, when you started, I instructed her to provide whatever you needed. Consider it an investment in my business. We owe it to our customers to use the products we sell and be our best examples. You look fabulous, Bree." She spun, turning her back to Bree.

"That outfit is lovely for the shop. The black sheath dress will do fine for dinner, but the houndstooth jacket is too businesslike for evening. I have just the thing." Opening her closet door, she pulled out a short, Kelly green, silk jacket. "Slip this on."

Putting a finger to her lips she studied Bree, as she slipped into the elegant jacket. "Um…not quite there yet. Remove those low-heeled pumps." Again, Mia dug into her stash, returning with black, strappy stilettoes.

Wiggling them in hand. Bree took the shoes and slipped into them. "Nice."

"Much better." Mya lifted Bree's curls from one side. "Those pearls will work, but the outfit needs something else." She turned and punched a few buttons on a small safe concealed inside the closet. "Here we go." She turned and held out a lengthy chain with a teardrop shaped pearl topped by a cluster of small diamonds. "Slip this around your neck."

Bree felt the finery of the delicate piece against her fingers and dropped it over her curls. The chain settled in her cleavage, and the pearl and stones centered her breasts like they'd found a cozy home.

Mya stood back and gave her another check. With a nod, she turned again. Spinning back around she held out what looked like a broach with tiny pearls in a strip. She moved close and lifted the mass of ginger curls with one hand, so it nestled above her ear. She inserted the jewelry clip in Bree's locks to hold it in place. "There," she stood back. "Now we can see those darling earrings. They show off your sleek neck. Very nice. You're going to knock Rex off his heels. I believe you're ready."

"Thank you, Mya. I feel like Cinderella." Bree spun around and did a silly model pose. She hadn't felt so free and feminine since she'd worn her wedding gown on the day she had pledged her life to Oran.

A mistake. Was this?

"Except you're not required to be home at midnight." Mya winked and laughed. She tossed a small, black, satin clutch to Bree. "Put your essentials in there. I already inserted a pair of footies. One never knows when you might need to remove those heels. My feet hurt something awful after a night of dancing. It pays to be prepared."

"Thanks." Bree made for the door. "I didn't realize you were a girl scout."

"I'm no such thing, Dear; but I believe in being ready for anything." She waived her niece out of the door. "Go, be the belle of the ball."

Bree returned to her own office, feeling like she'd been released from a massive burden. Had she really been that uptight since leaving Oran? She packed her tiny purse and stepped into the hallway.

"Looking good there, gal." Kaylee shot her a smile from where she stood locking her desk for the night. "I'm out of here." As Kaylee left the office area.

A second later, Rex entered. His eyes went wide. "Wow. You look amazing." Out of uniform, he was even more handsome. Bree hadn't thought it possible, but the black suit, grey shirt, and black pinstriped tie proved her wrong.

"You clean up rather well yourself, Chief." She grinned.

"Shall we go?" He put a hand to the base of her back and kept it there as they walked through the store. His touch burned a tattoo into her spine, sending delightful tingles of heat through her the whole way to the parking lot and his truck. He helped Bree in, the proper gentleman, held doors for her, and held her chair as she was seated at the restaurant.

"I hope you like steak. I'm a meat eater; but if you'd prefer, they have chicken and several fish dishes on the menu." He spoke over the elaborate menu, from across the linen clothed table. A small centerpiece held a lit glass candle holder surrounded with fresh flowers. The table was set with linen placemats, napkins and heavy silverware, and a stack of plates of varying sizes. Low lights lent the setting for romance, and soft music played in the background.

"I love steak. Thanks for asking." She opened the menu, noting there were no prices along the list of selections written in a fancy font.

A man in uniform strolled to the table, a linen napkin slung across his forearm. He introduced himself as the sommelier. "Will you be having wine with dinner?"

Rex looked at her for direction. With a tiny nod, she smiled; and he turned to the man. "We'll have a bottle of your house red, please."

Before she could decide on the ribeye or strip, the man was back with a stand holding a bucket of ice, their wine bottle encased in it. He slipped the flask out, laid it across his napkinned arm, and showed Rex the label. Rex nodded, and the man opened the bottle. He eyed the top half of it in the light, then poured a tiny portion into Rex's wine goblet.

Rex swirled the rosy liquid, looked at the glass, and took a sip. "Very good," he told the man.

The sommelier filled Rex's glass then hers, placed the bottle back into the ice bucket, and left them alone.

She took a sipped. Refreshing liquid coated her tongue with a delicate, fruity taste, going down nicely. "Yum."

A waiter arrived. "Have you decided on an appetizer?"

Rex glanced at Bree. She hadn't given it a thought. "Whatever you'd like is fine."

Rex pointed to a selection on the menu. "We'll have the fire-roasted shrimp skewers and stuffed mushrooms."

"Very well, sir. Are you ready to order, or would you like to wait for appetizers?"

Bree smiled across at Rex. "I'm ready if you are. That way we can concentrate on talking instead of the menu." Rex nodded, so she continued, "I'll have the Caesar salad and small ribeye with asparagus."

The waiter wrote on a handheld mini-iPad©. "Very well, ma'am. What can I get you, sir?"

Rex ordered the porterhouse steak, baked potato, and house salad with blue cheese dressing. The waiter took their menus and left them to talk.

"So, Rex, tell me how you ended up as Police Chief in Northern Kentucky." She clasped hands in her lap. The man was an enigma she wanted to explore, especially since he'd successfully charmed her aunt into a long-term friendship.

"Well, I grew up in the area, went to college at NKU, and was in ROTC. Cora and I knew each other since high school. We married our senior year of college. When we graduated, she went to work for Mya as the store opened. I went in the service. I did pilot training at Columbus Air Force base, so we were able to be together most weekends. After a year, I was sent to helicopter training in Ft. Rucker, Alabama. We didn't get to see much of each other then. I was reassigned; and after a short leave at home, I was assigned to Turkey for the remainder of my stint."

"Wow, that's a long way from home. So, you were there for three years?"

"Yep, and yes, far, far away."

"I take it Cora didn't want to live in Turkey?" She took a sip of wine. It sounded odd that Cora didn't move to be with her husband.

"She didn't want to live there. Women aren't treated with the greatest respect in that country. So, she stayed home. Mya needed her, and she wasn't much for travel. I knew that when we married. We got together on R&R for a week in Singapore each year. I was able to come home for the holidays the second year."

"So, I guess that explains why you and Cora didn't have any children."

"Right. We decided to wait until I was home, and we were settled. Once active duty was over, I returned home, took a job as a police officer, and you know the rest. Cora got sick about a year later and died within three months' time." His eyes diverted to the ceiling with an exhale.

She put a hand over his big, warm, firm one on the tabletop. "I'm so sorry for your loss." Grief showed on his handsome face, and she swallowed a lump compassion for the man. He recovered quickly and turned to her with a smile.

"Thank you. I'm finally able to get through the days without expecting her to be singing in the shower or grasping for a second coffee mug in the morning. It's been rough. Mya's been a big help getting me through it. They were very close."

"Mia speaks fondly of Cora." Her habit of doing math in her head for all manners of things put Rex at approximately thirty-three years old. She had recently turned thirty.

Rex sat back in his seat and smiled. "So, tell me about you and how you ended up a homeless vagrant blocking my street the other day."

She chuckled. "I did appear that way. Didn't I?"

He laughed. "I'm glad we had this time to work out our differences. I was mean as a snake in a chicken coop that day. I need to apologize for my behavior."

"Thank you. You were a little gruff." She laughed at his comical description.

"I am so sorry about that. It's not my norm to push my bad moods on others, especially attractive, young women in dire need of assistance. It's no excuse, but I had experienced a hell of a morning. Before I had my first sip of coffee, a four-car pileup on the expressway had me rushing out of the house. It was horrific. A family of four was killed, one young enough to be in a car-seat. It really got to me, seeing those kids like that."

She inhaled her surprise. "I'm sorry, Rex. I would've been worse than you were, had I been through that." *Goes to prove, there are two sides to every story.*

"Still, it's no excuse for making your day worse than it already was."

She couldn't argue that. At least he realized how he'd acted. That was a sign of maturity one didn't always find in a man, regardless of his age.

"So, tell me about yourself, Ms. Collins." He snickered.

"Let's see, I grew up in Hazard. It's a small mountain town in Eastern Kentucky. Mom and Mya were sisters, no other siblings. I went to EKU and met my husband there. Oran and I were married our senior year. We'd planned to wait until graduation, but my dad took ill, so we moved the wedding up so he could be there. He died not long after.

"I'm sorry, Bree." He frowned, and tiny wrinkles in his forehead and around his probing eyes helped make him even more handsome.

"Thanks. Only one of us could afford to go on to school. Oran went into law school, and I took a job working at an attorney's office in town. Mom moved in with us, and that worked fine, because Oran adored her. Everyone did. The idea was I would go back and get my MBA after he passed the bar. Once that happened, my pursuit of further education moved to when his firm was up and running. I became his Office Manager and helped him get the business started. He hired a couple more attorneys and a paralegals. Time just passed. I never made it back to school."

His brow furrowed. "But Mya said you have an MBA."

"Oh, I do. Now. I started noticing my husband was spending an inordinate amount of time behind closed doors with his paralegal. One day I caught them red handed."

His face took on a look of wonder. "You walked in on them? Fooling around? You'd think he'd at least lock the door."

"As Office Manager, I had keys to all the offices and file cabinets in the building and the combination to the safe. I let myself in. Keys in one hand and my phone in the other. I caught him with pants around his ankles, her legs around his neck, and his piddly little dick stuck up her wazoo."

He laughed, then pushed a hand toward her. "Sorry, but that's actually kind of funny. I'm sure it wasn't at the time. What did you do?"

She snickered. "I snapped a couple of photos, said, 'Smile.' Then I told her she'd best see a doctor because Oran had syphilis. I closed the door; went to the safe and changed the combination; grabbed my computer with all the company files on it, and my purse; and left."

"Good for you. That sounds like a scene from a comedy." He shook his head, laughing. "Then what?"

"I went to the bank, took our funds out of our accounts, and closed them. I went across town and put them in a safe deposit box under my name only. Then I drove to the attorney I had worked for previously. He and Oran hated each other, and he'd beat Oran several times in court."

"Bet that pissed Oran off. Isn't it hard to get a good settlement out of a lawyer?"

She nodded. "Usually, I'd say that's true. When my attorney showed Oran the photos I took and told him I was ready to send them to the press and directly via email to his clients, Oran backed down. In the end, we settled without much squabble. I went back to school, got my MBA. Then Mom died, cancer. She went fast. I worked for a while for a PI in town, one we'd used at the firm. It wasn't what I wanted, and I didn't see a career for myself in Hazard. With Mom gone, there was nothing keeping me there. Mya kept insisting I come, so I finally took her up on it."

"Good for you. I love that you didn't let that little twirp get away with that. I like a strong woman. You're fearless." Admiration glowed from those gleaming gray eyes, and dimples formed in his square jaw as he smiled.

The compliment shocked her. "I haven't felt that way. I sure as hell didn't act that way when we met."

He laid hands on the table. "Listen, let's chock it up to both of us having an extremely unusual amount of stress to deal with that day. Let's forget it."

"Good idea." She exhaled what was left of self-resentment from her ridiculous portrayal of a dopey damsel in destress. Hating the idea of helplessness, her actions the day they'd met had left a lingering, bitter flavor in her mouth.

He reached for one of her hands, and she allowed him to take it. It felt safe and warm, nestled in his big mitts. His brows rose. "You are fearless. You put that man through school and helped build a successful business. Then you tossed him on his ass when he didn't live up to his end of the bargain. You didn't let him push you into settling for less than you deserved and went back to school to do what most people never will. You cared for your mother through a devastating illness, and you left everything familiar to pursue a new career in a town where you knew only one person. That's bravery in anyone's book."

Wow. She'd never summed it up so raptly. Funny how sometimes others see what one missed in themselves.

He pushed back from the table. Remainders of his steak a mass of bone, juice and fat, his potato a skeletal shell, and salad gone. "I'm stuffed. Would you like dessert?"

She glanced at her plate. The ribeye had disappeared without effort, leaving one lone asparagus as evidence of a meal. Her salad plate was mostly emptied. "No, I don't think I can handle anything more."

He signaled the waiter for their check and stuck his card inside. The man went to ring it up, returning quickly for a signature. Stuffing his card in a wallet, Rex turned to her. "Ready?"

"Yes, thanks." She stood, and he pulled her chair out. Again, his heated hand branded her back as they strolled to his ride.

Chatting pleasantly together, they learned they liked much of the same in food, music, entertainment, and sports. He wanted kids, and she liked him more than she'd expected to.

As he delivered her to her door, he took the key and unlocked it for her. He cupped the key in her hand, bringing her fingers to his lips. "It's been great. I enjoyed your company. Say you'll let me take you out again." He didn't wait for an answer. "Tomorrow is Saturday. How about I show you some things in the area you need to see and experience."

"That sounds wonderful. I'm working tomorrow morning. You can pick me up here at one?"

"Perfect." He released her hand, placed his on her shoulders, and gave her a slow, soft, peck on the cheek.

That simple act left her more turned on than if the man had given her a sensuous lip kiss with tongue and pressed himself against her with a hardon nudging her body. Her thong was wet, and it took ten minutes to get her breathing settled down after she slipped inside alone.

CHAPTER EIGHT

Bree looked at the stunning male beside her in the black, shiny pickup truck. If possible, he was even more handsome in jeans that showed off his tight rump and a grey tee shirt. Short sleeves revealed thick, muscular arms. Fabric laid across his chest like a soft caress, giving a heady sense of pecs hidden beneath.

"Where are we heading?" She turned toward the street.

Rex shook his head. "Not so quick. It's a surprise, but I promise you'll like it. Why do you think I grilled you at dinner? I wanted to know all the things you're interested in, what you are game for, and what you're not, so I could show you a good time. There's a lot to do around here, and I wanted to know what you might enjoy first.

She groaned. "Okay, but I never told you I liked surprises." It was sweet how much he'd focused on learning about her. It had been a long time since any man had paid so much attention to Bree.

He snickered. "You aren't opposed to them either, or you wouldn't be here now."

She had to hand it to him. He had a way of reading her actions and making her realize things about herself. Rex saw features in her she had ignored or not considered and brought them to light in ways that boosted her self-esteem without arrogance. Not only was their friendship growing by the minute. As she spent time with him her life expanded like a giant, hot air balloon. Her world was becoming infinite, limitless.

It was an intoxicating sensation, much like the man's unique scent. She wasn't sure if the smell of him was a selected fragrance or his personal aura. Probably a thrilling blend of the two. Whatever the combination, it sent steamy waves of delight through her that made her stomach giddy and playfully enticed her private parts.

They crossed the Ohio River and headed away from downtown, east up a hill, one of seven that populated the Cincinnati landscape. Rex turned into an entrance on the right. A sign read Eden Park. The two-lane, windy road passed a concrete pond. Children waded in and played around it, while adults supervised from nearby benches.

He pointed to structure on top of a knoll nearly hidden by trees. "That's the Cincinnati Art Museum. The Playhouse in the Park is behind it, where Broadway plays are put on. Sometimes there are outdoor symphony concerts, and people spread blankets or bring chairs to listen. The Cincinnati Art Institute is up there, an exclusive school. Only the most talented get in."

She wasn't opposed to teasing. "Impressive. I kind of like having my own tour guide. Do I have to tip you at the end of the day?"

He took her hand in his and held it close to his thigh. She was sure his warmth had marked her flesh, but it was a delightful sensation.

He winked. "We'll discuss that later."

They passed a glass, domed structure on the left. "That's the Cincinnati Conservatory. It's dedicated to growing the finest flowers. We'll have to go there sometime and wander through the jungle room and other inside displays. The smells are incredible, and blooms are epic."

She tilted her head, studying his strong face. "But not today?"

He grinned as they made another turn, keeping eyes on the road. "No. We have other territory to explore. In the winter on the other side of the Conservatory building, they create a life-sized nativity scene with live animals. It's worth waiting in line to see it up close. It will get you in the holiday spirit like nothing else. The pond we passed freezes over, and people can ice skate there."

A couple holding hands strolled along the sparsely occupied sidewalk. Eventually, the lane opened to a vast overlook.

He pulled the truck into a parking space near a picnic table. "We're here. Feel up to a short stroll?"

She glanced at her sneaker-clad feet and saluted. "It's a go. Walking shoes on, as requested."

He helped her out of the tall truck and took her hand. They walked slowly, chatting about one thing or another, through winding paths that weaved in and out of floral spaces, and around a winding brook and small pond.

An arched, wooden bridge spanned the brook at a narrow space. They stopped to lean on the rail and watch swans and geese swim.

"This is lovely. Thank you for bringing me here." Her eyes widened as a swarm of giant, orange, black, and white fish swam beneath the bridgeway. "Are those goldfish?"

He snickered. "Kind of. They're coy, a Japanese type of goldfish that grow large. He pulled a baggie from his tee shirt pocket, opened it, and handed her a cracker. "Break it up and toss it one piece at a time to the fish."

She did, and a massive golden coy with a black swatch across his face dashed to the surface, thick lips gobbling the chunk. "Wow. It didn't even have time to get soggy."

She crushed the rest and tossed the bits in all at once to the cluster of fish circling the winner of her prize. Heads bopped up. Gaping mouths went wide to consume every bit of her offering. A tidepool of water circled from their activity.

Rex dug into his pants pocket, pulling out a wad of change and handed her a coin. "Here, toss it in." To her worried look, he responded, "No worries. They won't eat it. Make a wish."

She closed her eyes and wished for a home and family of her own, a dream Oran had damn near destroyed in her. Then she threw the coin. It settled at the scummy bottom of the shallow pool along with many overs easily seen through the water.

She figured he'd ask, but instead he took her hand. "Let's go. I don't know about you, but I'm starved."

"Oh, where are we going for lunch?" The park had been nice, and she was eager to see more of it, but Rex had clearly planned a full afternoon for them. She couldn't argue the man needed to eat. Her stomach was ready to start growling like a lion.

"You'll see." His broad grin made him look like a giant kid about to give his mommy his first effort at a macaroni necklace.

When they reached the truck, instead of helping her in, he opened the silver toolbox attached in the truck bed and lifted out a large tote. "You carry this."

She took the bag, which emitted the most delectable aroma of meat and sauce, but she couldn't put her finger on what it might be. He turned again and produced a large picnic basket then shut the box behind him.

She followed him to a wooden table near the overlook, where he opened his container and whisked out a red, checkered tablecloth. He covered the table, then with a wet wipe from a package inside the basket, he washed the bench on one side. She put her package on the table and took the seat he had cleaned. Her stomach rumbled at the enticing scent.

Rex sat beside her and withdrew a bottle of wine and a corkscrew. Out came a couple of wine glasses. He uncorked the bottle, sampled it to ensure no cork was in it, and filled both goblets, handing one to her.

She sipped. "Yum." She gave him a sly wink. He'd obviously put a lot of thought and planning into this little surprise luncheon. She'd never been treated with such attentiveness before…not by a man anyway.

He handed her silverware swaddled in a red, linen napkin. Then he opened the bag she had carried. Out came three large containers and an assortment of small ones. As Rex flipped open each one, the fragrance escaped, swirling in fresh, spring air and making its way into her nostrils. Her belly growled audibly, and they laughed.

With a wide grin he met her eyes. "It's good I'm not the only hungry one."

She slapped a hand across her middle. "Excuse me. That was rude."

"Nonsense, I take it as a compliment to my choices. I got these delicacies from The Boathouse. It's a riverfront restaurant owned by The Montgomery Inn, famous for the area's best barbeque." He pointed to each box he'd opened as he spoke. "We have ribs sure to give you an orgasm, chicken that falls apart in your mouth, and their homemade onion straws." He pushed a massive pile of tangled, brown, crispy strings toward her. "Dig in." He sat the package of wet wipes between them. "You'll need these." Pulling out a couple of plastic bibs from the bag, he offered her one. "Probably a good idea to use these too." He held one across her chest and tied it at the nape of her neck. "I wouldn't want to ruin that pretty blouse."

It was an intimate act but innocent as well. His arms around her made her want bring her lips to his, so close to her it would barely take any effort. Instead, she breathed in his fresh breath, warm and inviting.

Longing for that kiss, she wondered if he would be up for it after she consumed what she intended to of the onion rings. The thought brought heat to her cheeks, and she briefly closed her eyes.

Withdrawing, his gaze had a knowing aura to it. "I hope you don't mind the onions. I couldn't resist."

Had he read her thoughts or shared a similar one? "Of course not. They smell amazing."

"They are." He went about tying his own bib on. "At least we'll both have onion breath."

At that point, she wouldn't have minded had he chosen to eat limburger cheese with her, though she'd never been brave enough to put that particular orally offensive delicacy to her lips.

They ate and chatted awhile, getting to know each other better, and finding many common likes and very few dislikes.

In awe of the scenery, she gasped between bites of delicious food. "This view is incredible. We can see the city to the right, and the curve of the river as it rounds the huge bend. It looks like huge steps leading into the water."

"That's Serpentine Wall. Labor Day weekend, a barge docks center of the river and shoots off fireworks to music by a local radio station. It's a massive party on both sides of the river. Stadiums line the riverfront, and when the Reds hit a home run, they let off fireworks."

She pointed toward town. "There are so many bridges, a yellow one and a purple one."

"The yellow one is I471. The Purple People bridge is for walking. We will do that sometime."

It wasn't offensive, the way he imagined they'd spend more time together. His assumption was what she been hoping for. She eyed him critically. He acted as though he was enjoying himself nearly as much as she.

Everything around her seemed larger, more impressive than what she'd been used to. "The Ohio River is so wide, compared to anything 'down home.' My hometown sits at the North Fork of the Kentucky River. It would take almost four of it to be as wide as this one."

He laid his rib bone down, snatching another hand wipe from the pack. "Maybe we can walk across one night and catch a free concert. The city puts them on frequently during summer at the P&G Pavilion this side of the bridge."

How could she resist? "That sounds fun. Make sure I know we're going to do that. I'd hate to be caught in heels for that long walk."

His eyes met hers. Adorable crinkles formed at the edges of his like delicate frames on an elaborate piece of artwork. Those baby grey eyes of his glistened. "I like that you seem game for almost everything. What about bungie jumping?" His brows wagged at the playful dare.

Her eyes went wide, and her chin shot back. "Not on your life, Big Boy. I cannot see myself dangling from a bouncy rope over something that might kill me."

He laughed. "Well, they do it off the Purple People Bridge. If we walk over, we can watch those more daring than us. So, would you consider zip lining? Sky diving? How about hot air balloons?" His head cocked to the side, appearing to study her reaction. The guy was giving it his all to find out what she enjoyed. She gave him credit for effort.

A thrill shot from her tummy upward. "Maybe ziplining if it looks safe. I can see myself flying over treetops. There's no reason to jump out of a perfectly good airplane. Hot air balloon? I'd have to know the pilot was skilled and get a good look at the basket and equipment before I set sail in one." There sure was a lot more to do here than in the hills of Kentucky.

He laughed then turned back to his meal, sampling chicken with gusto. "Great. Maybe we'll try jumping. There's a place in Northern Kentucky near the Creation Museum, where you can zip over forested hillsides and down toward the Ohio River near where I275 crosses to Indiana. Three casinos and Lawrenceburg Speedway are on the Indiana side of the river. There are also a couple speedways on the Kentucky side of the river."

She had read online about some events and places of interest in the Greater Cincinnati Area. "Someone said there's a museum built like Noah's Ark."

He helped himself to a slab of ribs and indicated she should do the same. "That's in Dry Ridge-Williamstown area. There's a great dinner theatre in that area and a rodeo palace that operates year-round. Cincinnati hosts a national rodeo and a circus once a year."

She swallowed the delicacy that melted in her mouth, leaving a sweet, savory flavor. "I've been researching. There are lots of things to do. Jazz, blues, and country music clubs, and every kind of cuisine I can think of. The Marine Museum is close to our shop, and I hear there are lots of museums in the area."

He picked up his wine glass with a nod. "There are. If you like history, there's the Taft Museum downtown, which houses some incredible artwork. The Harriet Beecher-Stowe House and The Howard Taft Museum sit on hills surrounding downtown. The Natural History and Children's Museums are at the old train station, Union Terminal. It has a surround theatre. The huge domed building is spectacular. Stand at one side of the arch and you can clearly hear someone at the far end talk, as though they were standing right beside you. Giant tiled artwork surrounds the ceiling of the enormous entry room. Much of it is now displayed at the airport; but several pieces remain intact, depicting evolution of area workers."

A gleam in his eyes as he spoke, shoulders back, he spouted a booming laugh every so often. Dynamic movement and an eager grin conveyed his excitement at sharing his knowledge with her.

She leaned in and couldn't take her eyes off him. Restlessness caused her to adjust in her seat; but she kept eye contact with the fascinating man, unable to wipe the ridiculous smile off her face.

"The National Underground Railroad is on River Row along with The Reds Hall of Fame. The Contemporary Arts Museum is downtown, and there are many more."

Her head was spinning, taking it all in. A breath rose to bottle up in her chest. Her limbs tingled with anticipation. She did not want him to stop. It wasn't what he said as much as the way he spoke and his obvious intention to show her a good time. "I hear the zoo is world-famous."

"Yes, it's on the north side of downtown, not far from here. Very fertile. It's known for producing exotic animal offspring never birthed in captivity."

Lightheartedly, eagerness to explore her new world grew with each word…with the striking policeman. "I'd love to see it."

Eye contact was intense, and he offered a satisfied smile. "Let me show it to you. It's a great way to spend a day." He stood and shoved his paper plate into the large tote.

She rose to her feet beside him and did the same, then put a hand to her middle. "I'm stuffed. That was delicious. Any chance we can walk this great food off?"

He stowed remnants of their meal in the sack. "I've got just the place." He tossed the empty wine bottle and food bag into a trashcan.

She wiped their glasses and put them and napkins inside Rex's basket. He returned, picked it up and took her hand. It felt oddly natural. She was becoming accustomed to hers being held by his larger ones. As his thumb caressed the top of it, tickles of pleasure zipped through her.

They took the truck to a hilltop and parked aside a Greek-styled, stone building complete with gigantic columns. "This is the Cincinnati Art Museum." So many things to explore, right there inside the park.

She laughed, and her face went into a smile that could not be contained. "I'm so excited. Thank you."

His square chin went high. The little cleft showed in it. "My pleasure."

They spent the whole afternoon exploring the nineteenth century building filled with over sixty-thousand masterpieces. As they drove home, she leaned her head against the headrest. Her body heated with pleasure of her hand in his and warmth coming from his thigh against it.

Her voice had a satisfied lilt she was unaccustomed to. "I'm overwhelmed, as much as I am exhausted. We saw things today I never thought to be near in my lifetime. Botticelli, Claude Monet, they were stunning. That building holds a wealth of historical and contemporary artwork I never thought could be in a single place. Ground-breaking photography, American Indian, European, paper, and musical art. Sculptures span from medieval times to modernism. The comprehensive collection of miniatures said it is the oldest Asian art collection in the United States. Diverse cultures—India, China, Japan, and even Tibet, among others. I can hardly believe I saw works by Vincent Van Goh, Henri Matisse, Pablo Picasso, French pastels by Edgar Degas and Piere-Auguste Renoir—incredible. Craftsmanship of Jean-Baptiste-Jacques Augustin took my breath away. They even have fashion and textile art by the finest designers ever—Gabrielle Chanel, Christian Dior, Halston, and others I can't recall."

He pulled into her driveway and put the car in park. "They do have an impressive, in-depth, and broad-ranging variety."

She could hardly contain enthusiasm. Arms animatedly whipped around with her words. "Yeah, it's unbelievable. Take that landmark Nancy Rexroth Collection, with a contribution of works by Virgil Ortiz and Maria Martinez. Over three-hundred Native American photographs of her works, even a complete set of Diana camera pictures from 1977 and 2017."

She had never felt so connected to the world around her. "I was astounded by architectural fragments, decorative arts, and paintings representing religions of South Asia. The Jain domestic shrine from Gujarat and paintings from the Mughal empire, fragments from the temple of Khirbet et-Tannur, along the ancient trade route of Petra. Outside of traveling to Jordan in person, it's the most significant collection of Nabataen material in the world."

Her thoughts were scattered, almost too excited to think straight. "Thank you for making this possible. Just think. We were in rooms with antiquities from notable sculptors, decorative metalwork, painted carvings, and ceramic vessels from ancient Egypt, Greece, and Rome—places I never expect to visit. It almost inspires one to go the route of Indiana Jones."

He laughed. "Except, like Indy, I hate snakes."

Her face squirrelled up. "Yeah, me too. Where I come from, rattlesnakes and copperheads are everywhere. When I was a kid, Daddy woke up in the middle of the night, and a big one was crawling across the bedroom curtain rod. I heard the ruckus and ran in from my room. Mom told me to go back to bed. Dad had been having a nightmare, but I saw the snake he killed. Scared me so bad I didn't sleep a wink."

He cringed, as though picturing it and then nodded toward the house. "There's a light on."

She glanced at the second-floor lighted window. "Guess Mya is home from her date." Turning to him, she wanted his opinion. "What do you think of James Franks, or Jimmy, as Mya calls him?"

He pursed his lips and glanced up to the side and back, as though giving his utmost consideration. "Honestly, I don't know the man well. I see him at city functions and such. He's a respected businessman, polite, well-spoken. When he has a point, he can be influential. Why?"

Manipulative?

"Mya is very taken with the man. I haven't met him. They have busy schedules. You know? She's going to invite him to dinner soon. Would you like to join us, whenever that is?"

His broad hand fingered a tendril of her hair. He leaned in and took an easy whiff of it. "Thank you. That would be nice if I'm not on duty when she schedules it. I'll take any opportunity to spend time with you. You're a captivating woman. I've been itching to touch these wacky curls of yours. They seem to have a life of their own. I was wondering if they felt as soft as they look. They smell sweet, like you." His words grew softer by the word. He bit his lower lip and moved closer.

She swallowed hard, entranced by yearning in his voice. Her heartbeat pounded against her chest, as though trying to escape its confines.

His eyes seemed to glow from an inner light. Tiny beads of sweat cropped up on his brow.

Heat radiated through her body. Her chest rose and fell with deep breaths.

He licked his lip with a longing look. Eyes focused on her mouth. Unwittingly, her tongue slipped out and traced her bottom lip. His hands went to cradle her face between them, and he leaned in.

First came a gentle peck to the side of her mouth. Her eyes closed, and he kissed her lids then the other side of her lips. Finally, softness of his kiss met its target.

Tender at first, barely making contact, then harder he pressed with easy movement that captured her wits and drew her into its passage, shifting as one. His tongue slid out. Her mouth opened without effort, drawing him in like air she needed, as though joining in this intimacy with him was vital to survival.

Her mind went on automatic, acting on sensations, and forcing her arms around his neck. Fingers spayed into thickness of his dark hair. It was silky and tickled her palm.

A moan sounded. Which of them had it come from?

Slowly, as though reluctant, he eased away, and released her from the spell. She couldn't control the smile plastered on her face. Racing pulse and a fluttering stomach told her she was alive. More alive than she'd ever been. More aware, as though every sensation was heightened by their brief interlude. As though that kiss had changed her somehow, making her more of everything good about herself. A hyperawareness of her being and everything around her. Her hand rose, and back of her fingers slid down his wide jaw sending a tingle first to her heart and spreading downward.

A silly grin spread across his face, like a teenaged boy receiving keys to his first car. His words came out almost tongue-tied. "I'd best get you inside. It's getting late."

She nodded without speaking. As he hopped out and rounded the vehicle to open her door, she gathered her purse. He took her hand, helping her out of the truck, and shooting a jolt of electricity through her. She stepped down with care, fearing her legs might buckle under her weight.

As they walked to the door, he rested a possessive arm around her shoulders, darting glances at her. His face flushed, and he gave a nervous-sounding laugh. She handed him her keys; and he unlocked the door, turning the knob and opening it slightly.

Her body leaned toward him like a magnet drawn to another. He moved close, so close she felt his breath on her face. His head tilted down, and he played a soft kiss on her lips. Not a deeply passionate one like they had shared in the truck, but a feather-like promise of more to come. Then he released her and stepped away.

He spoke with a higher-than-normal tenor, "Good night," and then turned and walked away.

As much as she wanted to stand there like a schoolgirl to watch him walk and drive away, until he disappeared down the street, she forced herself inside.

"Goodnight," she whispered to the air.

CHAPTER NINE

The following day Bree returned to the shop after lunch with Rex. As she put her purse into the closet in her office, Mya strolled in. "How was your date with Rex?"

"Oh, it was just lunch at the chili parlor." She looked up. Had it really been their second date? She hadn't meant their going out to be dates, only a way to get to know her aunt's friend. Clearly, Mia considered it dates. She'd gotten the date vibe from Rex also. She was being ridiculous. She was a grown woman, not some giddy teenager mooning over her first real date.

"What did you think of our Cincinnati style chili?" Mya's voice held a whimsical tenor.

"It was everything ya 'all told me it would be. The aroma hit me in the face like a thick blanket of savory goodness, as we entered. We had four-ways with beans, no onions and cheese coneys without onions. Rex ordered and said he didn't think our customers would appreciate our having onions today."

"Certainly not." Mya laughed. "The smell of chili on your hair and clothing is quite enough. You might want to spray some of that fabulous perfume you picked out before going back to the Cosmetics Department." She stood by Bree's desk. "So, did you like it?"

"Absolutely. It was amazing. No other word for it. I can see why ya 'all said I'd love it or hate it—no in between."

"You and Rex are spending a lot of time together." Mya's tone didn't imply opposition to the idea.

"I've been surprisingly enjoying his company. He's a delightful person, once you get past that hard, policeman persona. He said to tell you he's sorry he can't join us at dinner with Jimmy tonight. He's on second shift."

"No problem. As a matter of fact, Jimmy called a few minutes ago. He finally got the permits he has been waiting for, and his people are breaking ground tomorrow. He has a ton of work to do. He told me to apologize to you. He really is anxious to meet you. We'll do it another night later in the week once things settle down for him."

Bree shrugged. "Oh, sure, no problem. Maybe Rex can join us then."

"Sounds good." Bree followed Mya toward the door.

"Want to grab dinner somewhere fun this evening?"

"Sounds good. I've been wanting to try that German place down the street. Authentic German food sounds intriguing."

"Oh, that sounds delightful. They make the brew the best beer." Mya smiled, waved at Kaylee and went into her office.

Bree shut the door behind her aunt and went to spritz perfume and disguise the chili scent she was wearing.

♥♥♥♥

At seven that evening, Bree followed her aunt to the parking facility. Mya tossed keys to her. "You've been thinking of buying a new vehicle. Drive mine. You might want one, and I'm bushed."

Catching the key chain, she studied the Mercedes® emblem on the soft leather strip. "Are you sure? It's an expensive vehicle, and I've never driven one before." Bree hit the button, and a beep sounded as the doors unlocked.

Mya climbed into the passenger seat. "Honey, cars are to be driven. No worries. They didn't quit making them."

Bree settled her behind into buttery soft leather. The tan seat melted around her as though made for her tush. The car smelled of newness and elegance. As she backed it out of its space, it handled like a dream. There was something to be said for a fabulous car.

Her chest rose, and shoulders automatically flipped back. Chin high, a feeling of elation settled over her. "I'm not sure I can afford one like this, but it's certainly worth looking into. Now I understand the attraction."

Wearing a satisfied grin, Mya watched buildings span by the passenger window in slow traffic. The street was lined on both sides with interesting venues, restaurants, and entertainment. At a standstill, awaiting other automobiles to pull into one lot or another, Mia remained patient. Growing accustomed to traffic, she no longer felt like a complete newbie. Two vehicles stood between theirs and the lot they needed to park in on the left.

A gasp from Mya sent Bree's eyes following her line of vision. A picture window fronted an exclusive, romantic, dimly lit restaurant. A silver-haired gentleman sat at a front table, illuminated in candlelight. He was intent on conversation with a dark-haired woman.

Her backless dress exposed pale skin. Thick, raven curls were arranged in a chignon on the back of her head. Her long neck sported a necklace strand that caught the dim light.

As they watched breathlessly, the man reached across and took the woman's hand. She leaned toward him and allowed him to hold it on the tabletop.

"Jimmy," Mya's voice was but a whisper.

Bree sighed her worry out and tried to put a spin on it. "Mya, it's probably not what you think."

Mya didn't meet her eyes, seemingly spellbound by her lover with another woman. "It's exactly what I think. No man takes a woman to a candlelit dinner in a fancy restaurant and holds her hand while they talk business. Working late, my ass. That fool is stepping out on me. He's going to be sorry we ever met." Her face turned toward traffic in front of them. "Get me out of here before I make a public spectacle of myself by meeting Jimmy's new bimbo."

The weasel in the window might've used her aunt to help him get in with influential people in town, to make his business life easier, and possibly more lucrative. It was well-known Mya, and the mayor were friends. She'd known influential members of the City Council most of her life and was a respected member of the business community. "When did you start dating James Franks?"

"Soon after I bought my house across the street from his. The subdivision was nearly finished, and most homes had been sold. That was a little over two months ago." Mya spoke quietly, staring at the bumper of a vehicle in front of them as Bree pulled out into moving traffic.

So, that wasn't it. He must've liked Mya for the wonderful, generous woman she was. "You didn't by chance invest in his next venture. Did you?"

"Heavens no. We never even spoke of that possibility. James handled his work, and I did mine. We didn't try to interfere with each other." Her sniff was barely audible.

Periphery vision showed Mya dabbing her eyes with the back of her hand. It seemed best for Bree to leave it alone and let her aunt grieve the loss of her love life in her own way. She focused on driving until she pulled the Mercedes into the garage. "You know, I just might go check out one of these babies. It's a dream ride and fun to drive." She was glad to have another topic to talk about.

Mya patted her hand and accepted her keys. "You do that, Dear. One must provide what she wants on

her own. A gal can only truly depend on herself. If
you want something, go get it. Don't ever let a man
hold you back or say you can't have it or don't
deserve it."

What had happened to make Mya so cynical and
independent? Her aunt unlocked the house, and they
paused in the kitchen. Bree took a seat at the bar,
considering what to do next.

Mya pulled a fresh bottle of wine from the
refrigerator. "There's a half bottle of vino in there for
you. I'm going to need this one. Lasagna is left over
from a couple days ago. It should still be good if you
want that for dinner." Mya was obviously making her
dinner that bottle of vino.

Bree watched her beloved aunt fish in a drawer
for the corkscrew. She found it and forced it into the
stopper, yanking it out with force that made a small
pop. "I won't be needing that." She gave Bree a sad
smile, tossing the cork into the trash and shoving the
opener into the drawer it came from. Clearly, she
intended to finish the bottle off.

Mya fished for two wine goblets, sat one in front
of Mya, and held the other upside down in her hand.
"I'm taking dinner to my room. Don't wait for me
tomorrow. I may go into the office early, depending
on how well I sleep." She walked around as she spoke
and pecked Bree on the cheek.

"I wish there was something I could do to make
this easier for you." Bree hugged her aunt.

"No worries, Dear. I'll take care of it." She
winked, still looking down in the mouth then spun
around and started toward the steps.

Bree followed Mya up the stairs. "I'm going to
have dinner in my jammies."

CHAPTER TEN

The following day Bree pulled the last glitzy compact from the carton with the Pampered Tigress logo on it and slid it into place on the shelf. Kaylee rushed into the Cosmetics Department and to her side. She spoke close to Bree's ear, so she was the only one to hear, "Come quick. Mr. Franks is in Mya's office. They're having a shouting match. She's going to need you when he leaves."

Bree glance to the Department Manager. Corina Wilson had just finished ringing up a customer. "Corina, I'm needed at the office for a little while." Only a couple of shoppers were milling about the shelves perusing expensive merchandise.

Corina looked up from the register. "No problem. Take your time."

Bree was already following the quickly moving Kaylee out the open doorway and to the office suite. Soon as the door closed behind them in the office atrium where Kaylee's desk sat beside her boss' door, the rumble of angry voices filled the space, coming from behind Mya's closed door.

What exactly was being said wasn't clear. The tone told the story. Kaylee may not have a clue. Bree, on the other hand, knew the gist of the conversation.

Kaylee took her seat at the desk. Her effort to appear to ignore the row happening on the other side of the wall behind her was nervously ineffective. Bree's heart went out to the poor gal, unsure what Mya had shared with Kaylee.

Bree wasn't about to spill the beans about Franks' cheating. It wasn't her story to tell. She sat quietly in one of the guest chairs messing with her manicure. Hopefully her aunt wouldn't be overly torn up after the conflict.

The door opened. Kaylee and Bree's heads turned to the newest arrival. Andy Simms, a package courier carried a small carton inside. He smiled. "Hello ladies. How's it going?" He placed the box on Kaylee's desk and shoved a clipboard toward her. "Sign here."

Kaylee acted relieved to have something else to concentrate on, even for a brief second. She took the pad and signed her name then handed it to Andy. "We're all good here."

As Bree answered, Mya's door flung open; and her aunt stepped to hold it with her rear. Arm's crossed, she glared at the man inside. "Now, get your sorry, two-timing slug of an ass out of my store. Set foot in it again, I'll have you arrested."

James stepped past Mya; handsome brow furrowed. "Now, Mya, Sweetheart. Don't be this way." His words were futile.

Mya didn't seem to register them. "Stay far away. Come near me, you'll be sorry you and I ever met." Her head whipped around to her assistant. "Kaylee, please call Albert Bane."

The situation didn't warrant involving the store's Head of Security, from Bree's perspective. It was probably just Mya's way of making her point with Franks.

Kaylee moved in a flustered manner, reaching for the phone as though wary of making the call. Before she could dial, James rushed past with a 'humph.'

He strutted to the exit door. "No need. I'm leaving." His head shot back to Mya. "Call me when you cool down." The door shut behind him, as he disappeared into the store.

Mya gazed at Kaylee. "Make sure he leaves."

Kaylee stood and walked to the exit then into the store.

Bree didn't stand. "You okay? Need to talk?"

Mya snickered. "You really are a doll, Bree. Nope. I'm fine. Glad that's over." She casually turned and went back to her desk, leaving the door ajar.

CHAPTER ELEVEN

Appropriately, the weather complied for gloominess by supplying a light rain, which wasn't needed. Saturated soil from the last bout of spring rainfall seemed right for what Mya was going through, though she was a trooper and refused to show her pain.

Things were easy and quiet that evening at home. No talk of romance or the striking James Franks. Bree didn't bring up her budding romance with Rex either. The two women talked about work and sights Bree wanted to see or that Mya thought she should explore in the area. One would never know the woman had broken up with the only man she'd taken seriously over the last decade.

After an early night, Bree slept soundly and awoke at six-thirty. She jumped into her workout clothing and ran downstairs.

A note laid beside the coffee pot. "Couldn't sleep. Gone in early."

Coffee was thankfully, still hot. After a quick cup of Joe, Bree set off on her jogging route.

A large dumpster had been left by the burnt-out lot on the corner. A couple of city workers in blue uniforms were picking up debris and tossing it into the large, metal container. It was about time they cleaned that eyesore up.

Taking it easy the first couple of blocks, she allowed her muscles to warm and reached the end of the subdivision to turn left. Sticking to the side of the two-lane road, she jogged at a strong pace along sidewalks. Soon the wooded area on her right opened to land James Franks planned to excavate. His heavy equipment remained idle, when it should be hard at work, now Franks had necessary permits.

Upon approach something looked different. A closer look sent her heart plummeting like a bolder off a cliff. A body hung from the crane.

The large machine's tall boom held a thick chain with a clamping hook at the end of it, as always. Today, that hook was a bit lower than before. What looked like a body hung from it.

She raced across the road. She'd chosen the lane to jog along because of its low-to-no traffic. Today she wished there were more cars going by; but then again, that was probably why whomever had strung the man up there had chosen this spot to do his handywork.

Please let it be ana effigy of some kind. Please. Please.

No use praying. No such luck. A closer look proved the dangling bundle to be human.

Bree didn't want to step in the mud and leave footprints, so she kept to the blacktop roadway. Heart racing, blood rushed from her head. Her hand snapped the phone off her waist. She speed-dialed Rex's number.

Recognizing clothing on the corpse, her eyes closed, and head rocked back. The body wore the grey suit. Lap of the trousers were splattered red. No tie. The white shirt had been splattered with blood. The greying head of thick hair tilted toward her so she couldn't clearly see the bulging face. One black shoe was missing. A pink silk scarf tied around his neck connected him to the boom's hook.

Strangely, fingertips appeared bloody, as though cut or bludgeoned; though she didn't want to disturb evidence by trudging through the mire to get a closer look.

There should be a blood pool in the muck beneath Jimmy's body.

Her finger hit SEND. Rex's voice held a happy lilt. "Good morning, Bree. What warrants a call from you so early?"

"I...I ah...found a body. James Franks is dead." She gulped down a lump blocking her air.

"He's hanging from a machine at his construction site. You'd better get over here." She blinked to alleviate her brain's inclination to spin out of control. She'd never seen a dead body outside of a casket, except when her parents died. One had time to prepare when attending a funeral. This was not that, and her body reacted in a way she had to work at calming.

"Jeez." He sighed with a huff. "Don't touch anything. I'll be right there."

Bree paced, attention diverting and back. The corpse drew her eyes again and again. Thoughts rambled through her brain. How would Mia take this? Bree would have to be the one to break it to her.

Moments later, sirens wailed. Police vehicles came from every direction and blocked the road, keeping at bay potential traffic far enough away to protect an ample perimeter. Local news media vans pulled to the line of black-and-whites. People stepped out, some with microphones. Others with cameras. A lift attached to one news vehicle, took a camera-laden gent high enough to get a decent shot with a strong lens.

They must've heard the alert on the police scanner. Bree tried to ignore them.

Rex joined her, as other policemen and women began stringing yellow tape to keep onlookers away. "How are you doing?"

She frowned. "Good as can be expected."

Sympathy showed on his face. She had an urge to throw herself into his arms, but this wasn't the time or place. His people wouldn't understand. Far as they knew, she could be the culprit who planted the hanging piñata.

"Did you walk on the dirt? Touch anything? See anyone?" Adorable lines formed around his eyes.

She resisted stroking his jaw. "No, I stayed on the road. I was the only one around when I got here. No traffic since. The body was like that when I found him. I think it's James Franks."

"Okay, let me get my people going here. Then I'll take you home. Otherwise, the press will hound you all the way."

"Yeah, thanks. I need to be sure before I go home though. If it's Franks, I need to tell Aunt Mya."

"Yeah, sure." He turned and walked to a group of officers beginning to examine space around the body. Carefully, he stepped into areas where no tracks had been made. After a good amount of time, as the pros rushed around doing what they were supposed to do in such situations, Rex finally returned. As he finished taking e Bree's official statement, an unmarked white van showed up.

A policewoman lifted the chain to let a tall, thin woman probably in her forties, inside the area. Two men wearing white coveralls followed the female, walking directly to the body.

Rex put a cool hand on her forearm. "I'll be right back." He went to speak with the tall gal. After a while, he returned. "Okay, let's go."

He led her to his vehicle and opened the passenger door. She climbed into the truck, then he went around and joined her.

As he started the engine, he glanced toward her, took her hand, and squeezed it. "That's the coroner." He nodded toward the strange female."

"And the body?" Her eyes were intent on his.

"It's Franks." He pulled away and drove toward her street.

"Not suicide." Dread nearly choked her voice.

"No. How did you know?" His forehead wrinkled as he glanced her direction then back to the street.

"Too high. Nothing to climb on to jump off. Bloody fingertips. Tortured." She sighed and focused on getting the data out.

"Smart lady. It looks like he was tortured and then hung." His brows rocked up and down.

She nodded. "Yeah, but he wasn't tortured there. No blood pool, only splatter on his lap and shirt." Trouser legs didn't appear to have blood on them, from what she'd seen.

"Observant." He pursed his lips and continued staring at the road.

She stared out the window. "I learned a thing or two, working for a PI back home."

"Is Mya home?"

"No, went in early." It would've been easier breaking the new to Mia at home.

He pulled into their driveway. "You okay? Okay to leave you alone here?"

They were far from the press and Rex's police force.

Alone?

She turned, and her hand raked his square jaw. Prickles of an apparent quickly shaved beard tickled her palm. "I'm good. Thanks for caring."

"Alright then, I'll come see you and Mya later."

She leaned forward and gave him a soft kiss, drawing courage and strength from his taste. "See you later." She hopped out of the truck and went inside.

CHAPTER TWELVE

Mya's assistant busily worked at her computer as Bree entered the business suite. "Does Mya have important appointments today?"

Kaylee Armstrong looked at her calendar. "A buyer at three and a meeting with department heads at six, but that's just a regular update. Why?"

"Cancel her appointments and tell everyone you'll reschedule their meetings soon."

Kaylee eyed her with a curious expression but didn't ask. "Okay." She picked up the phone to do as she was told.

Bree knocked. Mya's voice was cheerful through the closed door. "Come in." Bree opened it, slipped inside, her heart heavy.

Mya smiled from her glass-topped desk. Her expression flipped to concerned. She stood and walked toward Bree. "Are you okay, Dear?"

Bree took her hands and led her to the couch on the opposite side of the room. "No, something has happened. Let's sit."

Mya's brows rose. Her mouth opened. "Oh, Dear; what's going on, Bree. Don't tell me. You and Rex had a spat?"

Taking Mya's hands in hers in Mya's lap, it was all Bree could do to keep tears from choking her words. "No, Mya. It's about Jimmy. He's gone."

Mya's head tilted. "Gone? Gone where?"

"He's dead, Mya. I'm so sorry. Jimmy is dead." Bree inhaled deeply allowing her shoulders to rise to take in much needed air. She needed strength. Maybe she could draw that from oxygen.

Mya's face winced up. "No. Bree, this must me a mistake. You're mistaken. Jimmy was just here yesterday. He's fine." She waved a hand as though that showed Bree's error.

"No, Mya. I found him myself. I saw his body. Jimmy is dead."

"Found him? Where? How?" Shock caused Mia's voice into a giddy stammer. She squeezed eyes shut, spreading fingers against her chest. Her pitch rose with every word. "That's impossible."

Bree used a tone she normally reserved for children, as though kid gloves might make it easier for her beloved aunt to understand and bear. "It's true, Mya. I found Jimmy hanging from a piece of equipment at his construction site."

Mya's hand gripped her neck. Her head tilted. Brows furrowed. "Hanging?" She reached for the remote on a side table and flipped the television on the wall opposite them on and spoke as though trying to make Bree understand. "That's ridiculous. If something had happened, it would be all over the news. I've heard nothing."

The blonde news reporter Bree had seen at the scene came on the screen as the TV came to life. Mya sat transfixed by the screen. The crane was visible behind the reporter, and a group of police officers were doing their jobs. "We have yet to receive an update from the police. They have been working diligently at the scene. A body was discovered this morning by a jogger. The construction crew that was to begin excavation of this property for the James Franks Development Company arrived but were unable to begin work due to the ongoing police investigation. The body has been taken to the morgue. One crew member told us he believes the body to be that of the property owner, James Franks. He assumed it to be a suicide."

Mya gasped then quieted to listen to the remainder of the report.

"We will have further information for you once we speak with the police force. It is my understanding they will hold a press conference later this afternoon. Back to you, Bob." The camera switched to a correspondent at a desk.

Mya switched it off and spoke as though offended. "That's the most ridiculous thing I've ever heard. Jimmy would never commit suicide. The man is Catholic, for Christ's sake."

Bree stared her in the face. "He did not commit suicide. The body was his, but there is no way possible he could've hung himself in that manner. I saw myself. He was hanging by something pink that resembled a silk scarf."

"Pink?" Mya's eyes winced.

"Yes, pink; and his fingers were bloody nubs."

Mya's nose screwed up. "Bloody? You mean he had been in a physical fight?"

Bree shook her head solemnly. "To me, it appeared he was tortured. There was no blood at the scene, only a little on his clothing. He was wearing the clothes he had on yesterday when he was here."

Mya's eyes widened, and her voice was shaky and soft. Halting, she spoke, "Why…would someone…do that to him? I just don't understand."

"I don't know, but I called Rex. He and his people are working on it. I'm sure they'll find out."

"I need to go there." Looking lost, Mya kept squeezing her eyes shut, as though trying to block out visions Bree's news had conjured up in her brain.

"No, Mya, we're going home. You're going to rest. Rex will be over later to talk with us."

Without argument, Mya grimly nodded and sat patiently while Bree walked to her desk, retrieved Mya's purse from the closet, and locked her computer away. Returning to her aunt, she extended a hand. "Let's go. I'm taking you home."

"But I have…appointments." Mya allowed her to lead her to the door.

"Not anymore. I asked Kaylee to cancel them for you."

At home Bree helped Mya into a sweatsuit and to the couch where she sat like a zombie waiting for strength to pull herself from the grave. She stared at the floor most of the day, intermittently sobbing into a tissue. Bree made lunch, which Mya refused to eat, and kept her supplied with hot tea spiced with Amaretto®.

When Mya wasn't looking, Bree kept an eye on activity happening across the street at James Franks' house. Mia needn't be aware of what happened there, consumed enough with grief without having another thing to worry about.

City workers at the burnout had been called off their job. Rex must've considered them to be in the way.

Police tape surrounded both lots. Uniformed men and women went in and out, sometimes carrying objects to or from the house. Occasionally, Rex appeared among them. She didn't want to draw attention to the organized chaos, for fear it would set Mya off on another tangent of bawling.

It was six o'clock before Rex finally showed up to talk with her and Mya. Bree answered his knock quickly, taking him aside in the dining room. "How's it going?"

His shoulders rocked up. "Slow. It's a huge task to collect all the evidence at the scene, and we had to go over Franks' house. I'm not sure when we'll be finished. How's Mya holding up?"

Bree shrugged. "Good as you'd expect. She was in love with the man. They might not have been getting along, but she wasn't over him by far. She's been crying on the sofa all day. I've tried talking with her, but she acted like she'd rather be alone with her thoughts. I made her favorite fresh chicken salad for lunch, but she wouldn't eat."

"I need to talk with the two of you together." His expression showed he hated this part of his job.

She couldn't blame him. "No problem. Let's get this over with."

They walked into the living room/ Mya's eyes rose from the carpet with a sad smile. "Hi, Rex. We've been expecting you."

He sat beside her on the sofa. Bree faced him from a chair to Mya's other side.

Rex smiled with sympathy in his eyes. "Mya, I'm sorry for your loss. I truly am."

She patted his hand, resting on his knee. "I appreciate that, Rex. Now, tell me what happened to Jimmy."

Rex's shoulders went back. "James was murdered."

"I get that, from what Bree told me. Why? Who? Bree said he was tortured, something about his fingers." Mya's eyes were huge.

Rex nodded without changing expressions. "It appears he was. We don't know why or who, but we've figured out where. His fingers were cut off, it appears, at his home office. Then he was hung by his neck at the construction site. Do you know of anyone who might want him dead or want something from him enough to use torture to get it?"

Mya's head shook. "No, I can't think of anyone who Jimmy had problems with and no reason anyone would want to do that to him." She burst into tears.

Bree handed her a wad of tissues. "I heard James arguing with the Planning and Zoning Commissioner. The County Clerk said they regularly argued and rarely got along, but they had to work together to get Mr. Franks permits needed to do his work."

Rex frowned. "I'll check that out."

Bree was happy to help but not sure it was enough. There had to be more to this.

Rex turned to Mya. "When did you last see Jimmy?"

"He was in my office yesterday." She sobbed between words.

Rex had a stern expression. "A delivery man came forth today, hearing the newscast. He said he overheard you and Mr. Franks arguing yesterday in your office. He claims you threatened Franks and told him he'd be sorry you and he ever met. I spoke with your assistant, Kaylee. She confirmed Andy Simms was there. They both witnessed the shouting match between you and Mr. Franks. She was worried about you."

Mya gasped, hearing her words put into such context. "Yes, we had words. I might've used those words, but that didn't mean I meant to kill him. I didn't want Jimmy dead. I loved the man. Still do."

"Mya's right," Bree interjected. "They had a lover's spat. Jimmy was stepping out on her. We saw him with another woman. She confronted him. They broke up over it, but Jimmy left acting like he meant to patch things up between them when Mya cooled down. She hasn't seen him since."

One brow rose as Rex turned to Mya. Did he not believe Bree? "Where were you last night?"

"Asleep in my bed." Mya shook her head, shoulders slumping and hands dropping to her side in obvious disbelief Rex might be accusing her.

Bree sat erect. "She certainly was. I can vouch for that."

"And you?" Rex eyed her.

"Here., I read for a while in bed then went to sleep around eleven."

Rex put hands on his knees. "So, you two are each other's alibis. You can see. I'm sure. You are persons of interest in this case." He pulled a plastic package from his shirt pocket. A folded, crumpled, pink, silky item was sealed inside. "Do either of you recognize this?"

Mya reached for it. "Yes, it's my scarf. I haven't worn this for...um...about a month or more. Come to think of it, I haven't seen it since I last wore it. Oh, yes. Jimmy and I had gone for a long ride in the country. I wore it around my neck. We spent that evening at his house. I might've left it there." Her face slightly pinked, but she kept a regal demeanor.

Reading between lines, her aunt and Mr. Franks must've undressed that evening, probably for sex. It was none of Bree's business. Rex's either. They were mature, consenting adults; and Mya, at least, was in love with Franks.

Mya's pink disappeared, and her face went white. "Is that—"

Rex nodded, taking the package from her extended hand. "It was used to hang Mr. Franks." He pocketed the packet.

With a gasp, Mya's hand shot to her throat.

Bree heard the exasperation in her own voice. "You don't seriously believe Mya could've done this."

Rex gritted teeth. "I didn't say that. I said you are persons of interest. I will follow every clue to wherever it leads, regardless of my relationship with anyone."

Bree got the message loud and clear.

Mya rolled eyes upward and back. "Well for heaven's sake. Of course. Isn't the spouse or lover always of interest…until you find the real suspect. The fact is neither of us could've accomplished hanging that man. He outweighed me by at least eighty pounds."

A snicker crossed Rex's still handsome face. "I suppose so, but together you might've managed it."

Bree gave a cynical laugh. "Yeah, we would've looked like a bumbling Lucy and Ethel. Rex, you must admit, it's not the type of murder a woman would stage."

Rex snickered momentarily, and his face grew serious. "Mya, we have been unable to locate Mr. Franks' computer. Do you have any idea where he kept it?"

Mya's head tilted to the side, and she took a moment to think then met Rex's gaze. "Jimmy was very security conscious and protective of his precious computer. It was with him always. He locked it in his vehicle trunk when we went to an event and brought it home with him. He never left it sitting out, no matter what. I'm not sure where he kept it when at home."

Rex nodded. "What about banking? Do you know anything about where he kept his money? All we found so far is a checking account at Sweetwater Bank and Trust, and it had a very small amount of cash in it."

Mya's eyes sparked. "Heavens no. I stayed out of Jimmy's business and financial affairs. However, he did brag when we first met that he had funded the purchase of this subdivision property, paid for excavation and development, and fronted the cost of building the event house, pool, tennis courts, and the model home, which he lived in, with cash. As he sold the houses, he should've recouped his initial investment and made a great deal of profit. I assumed he had a substantial savings of some sort, but he never mentioned it. He lived rather prosperously, wore expensive clothing, and drove a Jaguar®. His house is tastefully decorated with expensive decor."

"Yeah, about that." Rex frowned. "His home is furnished with rentals. He leased the vehicle. His house is financed to the hilt. We can't find any sign of savings, investment account, or sizable checking account. All he seemed to own would be his wardrobe."

Mya's brow furrowed. "Well, he just purchased that new property to develop. He must've put the cash into that."

Rex nodded. "Yes, we thought of that. It turns out Franks only put down a small deposit on the land as an option to buy, not to be called in until he sold twenty-five percent of projected homes to be built on it. Equipment sitting there was rented and has run up a considerable debt for its use. We have found no liquid assets."

Bree's mind was spinning on overdrive. "That's ridiculous. Clearly, Mr. Franks was financially affluent. You just haven't located his money."

Rex looked doubtful, pursing lips "If either of you think of something that might help locate his finances, please let me know right away. In the meantime, I'll investigate Bree's lead on the P&Z

Commissioner. Is there anything else you can tell me that might be of help?"

Bree's eyes popped wide. "Yes, James was with a strange woman. We saw them having dinner together in the Flamingo night before last at around eight o'clock. She had dark, curly, longish hair, wore a backless dress or blouse. They were holding hands over a candlelit table. You need to find that woman. Maybe this has something to do with her."

Rex wrote notes on his phone with a stylist. "I'll do that. In the meantime, if you think of anything else that might help, let me know." He stood.

Bree followed him to the door. He put a hand to her shoulder. "This means we're going to have to cancel out date for tomorrow night. We can't go out while I'm investigating this case. Besides, I'll be too busy to think of dating for a while."

Her heart sank, but she'd expected as much. "Just find out who did this. It wasn't Mya or me. Rex. Mya swears Jimmy wouldn't commit suicide. Besides, are you sure he died from hanging? Doesn't a hanging victim usually piss themselves, and shouldn't his face have been more…I don't know, bulging?"

"You've got a keen eye, Ms. Collins. I'm waiting for the coroner's report, to determine COD."

"Surely, you're not seriously considering Mya and I as possible murderers?" She frowned.

He shrugged with a blank expression. "You could've managed it together. Look, Mya has motive. You both have means. Don't take it personally. Mya's right. You're going to remain persons of interest, at least until we can prove you're not involved." He didn't appear convinced his words made sense.

She snorted, and her shoulders rose and fell. "Yeah, sure; and the Pope has a belly dancer tat on his ass."

That got a giggle out of him. "I can see that. Take care of yourself and Mya too."

"Yeah, you, too."

CHAPTER THIRTEEN

News reporters received a briefing from Chief Ayers but continued to speculate. "It seems a Bree Collins has been identified as the jogger who discovered the hanging body of James Franks at his construction site earlier in the week. Ms. Collins is the niece of the deceased's lady friend, Mya Landry, owner of the popular lady's store The Pampered Tigress. Both women are reported as Persons of Interest in the case. We have learned Mr. Franks did not commit suicide, as was initially suspected."

Shoppers at the store dwindled. Sales were down. Those that braved entering the shop appeared to be there more out of curiosity than to purchase. They asked about and watched to catch a glimpse of Mya or Bree in the store. Suspicious eyes were constantly on them, no matter where they went.

Mya entered the office suite carrying a coffee container. Kaylee and Bree looked up from their chat.

Mya's red eyes were swollen, and tears streamed down her face. "Son of a bitch, I can't even go out for a cup of coffee without being accused of something I didn't do. Everyone stares. People are snippy or keep an obvious distance. Even my server looked wary as he served me. A gal behind me made a snippy remark loud enough for everyone to hear, something about safety in numbers. What do they think I'm going to do, grab a total stranger and overpower them?" She looked down with a swish of an arm at her five-foot-two, petite frame.

Bree put arms around Mya, and Kaylee pushed a tissue box toward her. She took one and blew her nose.

Kaylee stroked Mya's arm. "People are just plain mean. We know you had nothing to do with Mr. Franks' death. It's just horrible the way you're being treated."

Mya sniffed in a strong breath, and her shoulders went back. "The worst part is it's hurting business. I don't know how long I can go on like this. If things don't pick up soon, this could severely damage the shop's future."

Deep-seated need to help her aunt had Bree's mind whirling. Ideas came and went. Some settled into place in a puzzle she intended to finish. "Mya, I have an idea." She strolled into her aunt's office. "Let's talk." Kaylee returned to her desk, and Mya followed Bree then shut her door.

Sitting at Mya's round table, Bree played hands on top. "It doesn't seem like the police are moving fast enough. They don't appear to be getting anywhere. I'd like to do some investigating of my own. I could put a few snooping skills I learned from the PI I worked for in Hazard to work here, if you don't mind."

Mya's brows squinched up. "But Rex—"

Bree's hand went up. "Listen, I have as much confidence in Rex Ayers' expertise at his job as you do, but he's hindered by red tape and procedure. I'm not, and I think his people are missing something key. Rex gets all pissy whenever I bring up an idea, like I'm interfering where I'm not wanted. We can't afford to let clues go cold and risk the murderer getting away—not when the authorities keep coming back to you and me. A little snooping around won't hurt anything."

Mia puffed out a breath. "Are you sure it's safe, Bree? I can't lose you too. You're the only family I have. There's a killer loose in this town, and no one knows who it is."

Bree smiled calmly. "Not to worry. I won't do anything that puts either of us in harm's way." Mia was Bree's only family, too. It was partly why she was so adamant about this.

"Okay, what are you thinking?" Mia bit her lower lip.

Bree hadn't been able to resist calling Rex earlier to pry. She couldn't get much out of him, but he hadn't minded sharing a couple things she could tell Mya about. "Rex told me something on the phone this morning. After talking with the waiter and maitre 'de at the restaurant where we saw Mr. Franks and that woman dining together, they are nowhere close to identifying her. They got a grainy shot of the strange woman as she entered the restaurant, but that's the only guest area with security cameras. She entered after James and joined him at his table. They ate. He paid the bill. They walked out, but no one knew if they left together or went their separate ways."

Mya's brows tented. "That's not much to go on."

"No, it's not. I'd like to talk with them myself. I think I can get farther than that with those people. Maybe I could learn who our mystery woman is. Would that be okay?"

"I suppose so; but whatever you dig up, you need to share it with Rex. Let him and his people do the dangerous work. It's what they're trained for."

She patted Mya's arm. "Of course, Aunt Mya."

Mya sat wringing hands a few seconds. "I have an idea."

That evening at seven Mya led Bree into the Taco Table restaurant. "My friend never misses Taco Tuesday's unlimited tacos, her favorite. There she is now, at her favorite table."

Aromatic flavors scented the air. Each breath was a savory delight to Bree's nostrils. "It smells yummy. I've never had authentic Mexican food."

"You're in for a treat then." Mya waved at the woman across the room whose greying head had popped up as they entered, a grin on her pleasant, slim face. Mya toddled away toward a tall, slim woman about her age with a messy bun on top of her head.

A waiter walked to Bree. "Table for two, senioritas?" His accent was real. So was his jaunty smile. The pleasant, short man dressed in a brightly colored, floral shirt, and black slacks.

Bree smiled. "We'll be just a minute, please." She followed her aunt across the plank flooring in the multi-colored, festive room. Walls displayed Mexican hats, striped blankets, painted bowls and plates, and various other kinds of Hispanic artwork.

Mya had been speaking with her friend and turned as Bree walked to them. "Bell, I'd like you to meet my niece, Bree Collins. Bree, this is my dear friend, Belle Singer. Bell is the City Coroner."

"How wonderful to meet you, Bree. Why don't you and Mya join me. Don't make an old gal eat dinner alone. I just ordered a drink. Oh, here comes my waiter now." She waved him over.

"Yes, Miss?" The same pleasant man asked the seated woman. Bree and Mya slid into chairs across the wooden table from Ms. Singer.

Mya took charge. "I'll have a Modela in a frosted mug."

Bree looked up. "I'll have a Dos XX."

"I didn't think you knew Mexican food." Mya eyed her.

Bree grinned. "I don't, but I do know beer."

They talked. The waiter returned with their brews and icy mugs, a tray of chips, and three bowls of salsa. He took their orders and left them.

Belle's head rocked to the side. "I'm glad we ran into each other tonight. I've been trying to come up with the gumption to give you a ring. I wanted to tell you how sorry I am about what happened with that poor Mr. Franks. I know the two of you were a thing, and it must be awful for you, especially with townsfolks whispering that you might've done the fella in. That's ridiculous. You could never hurt a fly. I know you couldn't inflict that kind of damage to anyone. Besides, he could easily overcome you, even if you were wielding a gun—not that one was involved, mind you."

"Thank you, dear. It's so sad." Mya wiped away a tear that started to fall. "I loved the man. I couldn't harm him, much less hang him. That had to be a bad way to go. I can't imagine watching him die."

"Oh, he didn't die from the hanging." Soon as the words were out of Belle's lips, she glanced around to make sure no one was listening. "Oops! I probably wasn't supposed to say that. It's not been released to the press."

Mya's voice sounded cynical. "What difference does it make? The media makes up their own story, anyway."

Bell's nose squirrelled up, but she didn't comment on newscaster integrity. It wouldn't be professional for her to do so. "I figured, since Bree here found Mr. Franks, you were aware. If she couldn't tell by looking, I'd assumed Chief Ayers would've at least told the two of you. I mean," she turned to Bree. "I heard the two of you are seeing each other."

Bree smiled sadly with a closed mouth. "We are. At least we were, before this happened. Things are on hold until this murder is resolved—assuming the police actually find the killer."

"The Chief is giving it his all."

Bree studied the woman. "What did you mean, he didn't die from the hanging? Was he shot or stabbed? I didn't see any sign of that at the scene, but I couldn't get super close to the body. There was no blood pool in the mud below him."

The coroner shook her head. "No, he died elsewhere and from a heart attack."

Mya gushed, "But...he didn't have a heart condition I was aware of."

Belle's lips squeezed together before speaking. "I could tell. He didn't. His heart simply gave out under the strain."

Mya emitted a choking sound. "From—"

Bree saved her the heartache of voicing the words. "Torture?"

Belle's head rocked in answer. "Clipping off one's fingertips is agonizing. The fingers contain tens of thousands of neurons, each one with receptors on a small surface area of skin called the receptive field. That is why the Japanese pulled fingernails out as a means of torture meant to get prisoners of war to talk during the big war. It hurts more than you can imagine."

Tears were actively streaming down Mya's cheeks. She kept sniffing. Bree pulled a tissue from her purse and handed it to her. "So, Franks died of a heart attack brought on by pain inflicted from 'clipping' his fingertips off?"

Belle nodded. "It appears so, though the weapon used has not been located. The police found his fingertips in an otherwise empty, fancy humidor on Mr. Franks' desktop. There was a considerable amount of blood on the desk also."

Mya looked up. "He died in his home office?" Belle nodded without speaking.

Bree chewed the side of her lip. "What do you mean clipped? That seems to be a strange term. Were they hacked or cut off with something like a knife, ax, or clever?"

Bell inhaled deeply then let the air expire. "No, they were clipped. His wounds were inconsistent with a single flat blade. I examined the digits from both sides, the part attached, and the sections removed. They were definitely cut from all around pressing in. An extremely thin blade came inward against the finger." She demonstrated by wrapping a thumb and finger around one of her own on her other hand, then squeezing inward.

Mya stared at the table a second. Then her eyes brightened. "James had a prized titanium cigar cutter in his humidor, which he always kept filled with expensive cigars. I personally gave him a full box a few weeks ago for his birthday. He could not have smoked all of them by now. He would never leave the humidor sitting open or let it get empty. He was proud of that cigar cutter. It was a valuable antique he had bought at auction at Christies®. It had belonged to Frank Sinatra. Didn't the police find it?"

Belle shook her head. "I'm sure they would have brought it to me to try. I've checked every type of knife I've been able to come up with, trying to figure out what was used. A cigar cutter might just be the perfect tool. I'll ask the Chief, to make sure."

Bree bit her lip "You know, the things done to James seem to be too much for one person to manage. I've been thinking maybe there was more than one culprit involved."

Belle's eyes brightened. "I can't say you're wrong."

Clearly, Belle had considered that. Bree leaned forward. "Did you find any fingerprints?"

Belle's head shook. "No, whomever did this wore gloves. Criminals aren't usually smart, but they were clever enough to take that precaution."

Bree stood. "I'm going to walk outside for a minute. I want to ask Rex a couple of questions he may or may not want to answer."

The waiter brought their food as Bree strolled away. Soon as she was in the night air, she hit send on Rex's speed dial link.

He sounded happy to hear from her. "Hey Bree, what's going on? You and Mya okay?"

"We are. Rex, I realize you can't answer everything I'd like to know about the ongoing case, especially since we're inadvertently involved. Perhaps you can tell me this. Did your people find a cigar cutter anywhere in James Frank's things?"

His voice had a questioning lilt. "No, should we have?"

"Yes, Mya said he had a rare, antique one once owned by Frank Sinatra. It was titanium and unbelievably valuable, and it was extremely sharp. It's my hunch it could've been used to slice off his fingers. James was fond of it. It should have been in his office in a humidor. Mya is certain that humidor should have been full. If you didn't locate the cutter, maybe the killer took it."

His tone had turned to stern. "Thanks for bringing that to my attention. It's good to know. We searched every inch of his house and the area where you found his body. We did not find a cigar cutter. Thank you, Bree. That's helpful. How do you know the humidor wasn't full?" Suspicion entered his voice with the last sentence. "You haven't been in that house, have you? It's cordoned off with crime scene tape. Stay out of there."

Hope eased into her heart, and his attitude squeezed the life out of it. "Just a hunch, and you're welcome." A mocking attitude coated the last word. If the police found the right person, and they took the cutter, it could tie them to the murder. "So, is it murder if James died of a heart attack?"

Rex hesitated as though deciding whether to answer or not. "Brought on by torture. That alone is intent to kill. So yes. There is a case for murder."

"Anything new on the dark-haired woman?"

"No, and we haven't located his briefcase, computer or money yet either. We're following up on the victim's relationship with the Planning and Zoning Commissioner. Thanks for sharing your insight on that."

At least he didn't discount her contribution to the case. She was desperate to push him toward someone, anyone but her and Mya. She frowned into the phone. "Too bad. That money has to be somewhere. Maybe the computer holds the key to where he kept his dough; or maybe the killer took it all—cigar cutter, cigars, computer, briefcase and money. He could've given it up under duress…before—"

Rex hadn't spoken to her with such impatience since the day they'd met. "Look, Bree, I know you're trying to help. You want to bring us something that will clear you and Mya. I'm warning you to stay out of this. These are brutal criminals, we're talking about. They would not think twice about snapping your pretty neck. I don't want anything bad to happen to you or Mya. Please, be patient. Let us do our jobs. We will get to the bottom of this. Stay out of it."

Patience wasn't her strong suit. Bree wasn't having it. No matter he thought her neck was pretty. As she spoke, her tenor sang up and down, unable to hide her agitation. "Listen, Chief Ayers, this concerns me and my aunt. Our lives could already be in danger, for all we know. How do you expect me to sleep at night? If there is something I can do to help find out what the hell is going on here, I'm going to do it. Don't go trying to tell me what to do. I haven't been in Mr. Frank's house, though if I had, it would not be an illegal search. I happen to know my aunt has a key, given to her by the deceased. That gives her a right to enter with his permission."

Rex sounded more sympathetic, as though he was trying another tactic to control her. "Lis is a legal matter. That house is off limits. You hear me? Off limits. I could haul your sweet, little tushy to jail. At least, I could do my job without worrying you're poking your nose where it doesn't belong. Stay out of this, Bree. I will not tolerate you interfering."

His pompous attitude made hair on the back of her neck stand up. "You are welcome for the valuable information, Chief Ayers. Now stick it up your tight ass." She clicked off.

Her phone rang again as she walked into the restaurant. She looked at the screen and refused Rex's call. Again, before she took her seat, she deleted another call from him. Turning her cellphone off, she took her seat.

"This looks delicious." She eyed the table filled with bowls of aromatic tomatoes, cheese, onions, peppers, salsa, some sort of cooked meat, and guacamole. She lifted the lid on a covered dish holding a stack of steaming taco shells. "Yum, I'm starved." She met Belle's eyes. "The police did not find the cigar cutter."

Belle nodded. "Thanks."

CHAPTER FOURTEEN

It was time to take the situation into her own hands. Why did she feel like a traitor? It was an individual's right and responsibility to take care of themselves.

Bree had put together a grainy idea of a plan. Sitting across from Mya after lunch, she drew a hearty inhale of courage. "Mya, we have to do something besides sit around and wait for the police to determine our fate and haul our asses into jail. I'm done with being a victim. I won't be one in this case, and I won't let you become one. The police believe you and I have something to do with Jimmy's death. Long as they can't prove we didn't do it, and they don't have proof of who did, we're the easy out. They have hit a dead end as far as the mystery woman is concerned and are getting nowhere with evidence uncovered at Jimmy's house and the location, I found him at. You and I need to find some way to steer them away in another direction."

Mya's eyes looked red from crying and stress of the situation. "I agree with you, Bree; but I don't have the foggiest idea what we can do. It's all I'm able to do to keep the store running."

Bree clasped her hands in her lap. "I worked for a private eye for a while before moving here. He mostly handled cases of cheating spouses and people falsely claiming to be disabled. Sometimes when he had several going at once I went out on sting for him, taking photos and watching persons in suspect. I learned a thing or two from my detective boss and developed a few snooping skills. A little digging would be harmless."

"I'm not opposed to you doing some digging, but don't put yourself in harm's way, dear. Let the professionals do the dirty, dangerous work."

"Not a problem, Mya. Who knows? Jimmy could've died from heart failure before he gave up whatever the killer wanted. If that's the case, we could already be in danger."

Mya's eyes turned down and her jaw dropped. Bree fought the urge to go to her and wrap her in her arms. Mya was trying her best to be strong. Everything she loved was gone or dying. Her sorrowful eyes met Bree's. "I know one thing. The media is ruining my reputation and my business. I can't show my face without people gawking, talking about me with not quite enough voices, or bluntly asking insulting questions about my relationship with Jimmy. It's appalling the way people are asking. At first, there was no one coming in the store. Shopper numbers are starting to pick up, but sales are way down. They're mainly here to get a glimpse at the lady killer and her accomplice."

Bree gave a cynical chuckle. "Not sure if it's good or bad for business. Maybe they'll buy something as a souvenir. I know what you mean about shoppers. People stare when I go into store area. Dirty looks, glares, I'm starting to feel self-conscious. I'm not going to sit around and put up with this. I have to do something."

Mya gave a tiny nod. "Alright, Bree, but be careful."

She stood to go. "I will. Is it okay if I take the afternoon off?"

Mya spayed her hands on the desktop. "I suppose so. Charlotte can cover for you. She won't mind. It's unlikely we'll have a sudden influx of buyers."

Bree left her aunt with a pile of reports on her desk to keep her busy. She drove home and rustled through her unpacked items in a closet, locating a small wallet.

Flipping it open revealed identification her PI boss had issued to her to use in case she was questioned by a target or police officer while surveilling someone on his behalf. Boldly embossed in black ink on the laminated card's plastic cover were the letters 'PI.' Of course, it referred to her old boss, not her; but it explained why she was watching the target. It would have to do. She shoved the item into her purse.

No need to change clothes. The navy pants suit, white shirt, and navy flats she'd worn for work would look the part.

Chewing her lip, she studied the room. On a whim, she went to her lingerie drawer and pulled out a fresh pair of panties then tossed them into the bottom of her bag. One never knew...

Satisfied, she set out about her mission. First stop, the restaurant where Jimmy had dined with the dark-haired, mystery woman. The police hadn't gotten far with this lead. That didn't mean Bree wouldn't.

Personnel busily darted from place to place, some working at tables. The matre' de stood behind his station, sanitizing menus. She gave him a proper smile and did the flip thing with her identification badge, not giving him much of a chance to peruse it before stashing it back in her blazer pocket. "I'm Bree Collins, following up on the police investigation concerning the last evening James Franks dined in your establishment."

The man didn't appear impressed. Tolerant, maybe. His brows went up without eye movement, and he gave her a no-nonsense gaze. "Will you people ever get all you need? I've already told the other officers, Mr. James arrived alone. He took a table near the window. His guest showed up soon afterward, asked for him, I seated her. It's not my business to spy on our diner guests. They're paying for romance, elegant surroundings, impeccable food, and privacy. I leave them to it. My business is here at this station near the door."

He paused for a breather. "I suppose you want to see the tape again. As you probably already know, we only have surveillance here at the entry. Mr. Franks and his lady friend are only visible as they entered."

She allowed the slightest bit of compassion to coat her words. "Thank you, and I apologize for how we've managed to disrupt your work. I respect that you are busy and trying to ready the restaurant for the dinner crowd. I won't keep you. Is there anything specific you recall about either of them that evening?"

"No, Ma'am. Mr. Franks was his normal, pleasant self. He and the lady he dined with left at the same time. I have no idea what happened once they exited that door." He pointed to the ornate double doors at the front.

"Alright. If you think of anything pertinent, please let us know. In the meantime, I'd like another look at that security tape."

With a silent nod, he turned and walked away. She followed, and he led her along a hall to a door marked 'Private.' Opening it revealed a cubbyhole not much larger than a walk-in closet in the average sized home. A wall of shelving held electronic gadgets and rows of small boxes she assumed to be previous surveillance tapes.

He pulled a CD out of one and stuck it into a laptop computer sitting on a rickety, military, 50's style, metal desk. "The tape is still keyed up to where your people left it, so you won't have to search long. There's not much to it. Click here to roll the tape backward. Click this button to move forward. These two keys to slow or speed the roll up or down."

She took the wooden chair in front of the desk. Her feet barely reached the floor, making the seat spin automatically to its preferred position. "Thank you. I won't be long. When I'm finished here, can I speak with the person who waited on Mr. Franks and his guest that evening?"

He didn't bother disguising a low sigh. "Yes, he's in the kitchen. I'll tell him. Leave the tape in the computer. I'll put it away later." He spun, and the door shut behind him.

Clearly, they hadn't indulged themselves with the latest technology, and security wasn't of utmost concern for the restaurant. They must have bigger fish to fry.

The closed, dreary cubicle sent a claustrophobic tingle down her back. She forced herself to get the job done before the man decided to question her too intensely.

She flipped the screen on. A grainy photo of a forty-something, attractive brunette in a shimmery, knee-length dress appeared on the screen. She moved with confidence and dressed with class. Moving the tract forward and backward produced no better image. With her phone, she snapped a visual of the best view possible from what was available then clicked the screen off. As she stood to leave, a knock came on the door.

It opened to the pleasant face of a smiling, black and white uniformed waiter. "Thomas at the front desk told me you were asking for me. I understand you have questions." He leaned against the door jamb. "I'm Cary Adams, and as I told the police earlier, I waited on Mr. Franks the last time he was in. It's awful what happened to him." It didn't sound like the guy knew Jimmy personally. At best he'd miss Jimmy's impressive tips more than the man.

"Yes, it is. Anything you can tell me about that evening could be important."

He nodded. His eyes went up as though recalling details. Then he spoke toward the wall, like he was trying not to forget anything. "Mr. Franks arrived around seven. He was seated, and I brought him water. He advised me he was waiting for a friend. When I noticed a lady at his table, I returned and asked if they'd like a cocktail, wine or if they would like to order. Mr. Franks asked for wine and ordered the shrimp appetizer for two. He glanced at the lady, then smiled and ordered meals for both. They had lobster, rice pilaf and fresh vegetables. I left them, placed their orders with the kitchen, and sent the sommelier to their table. I delivered their dishes, replenished their water goblets, and after dinner, brought the check. Mr. Franks paid with cash, leaving a hefty tip. That's about it."

"Tell me what you can about the woman." She doubted Rex's people had gotten this much out of him.

The man shrugged. "I understand you have a photo of her. There's nothing more about her I could tell you."

"What about the way they interacted that evening?" This guy wasn't much help.

He shrugged. "I didn't hang around. We were busy. I was in and out but did not notice anything specific about either of them."

"The sommelier interacted with them. Can I speak with him or her?"

"Sure, come with me." He turned around. "Jeffrey is in the wine cellar."

Bree followed him to another room a tad larger than the surveillance nook. It was obviously temperature controlled, given cooler air in the space. "Jeff, this gal needs to ask you a few questions."

Jeffery turned from checking the ice machine. "Okay. Thanks, Cary."

"Mr. Adams, I appreciate your cooperation." She shook the waiter's hand.

He shot her a flirty grin, glancing at her ring finger as he took it. "No problem. I hope you catch the SOB who did that man in. He seemed like a good guy. Sure was a good tipper." Cary turned and left.

She focused on the restaurant's wine expert. "Jeffery, I don't want to take too much of your time and realize this is an inconvenience. I'd like to go over the statement you gave the police again."

Jeffrey looked confused. "I didn't give a police statement. They never asked to speak with me. I figured they had what they needed."

Bingo!

Bree pretended to read something on her phone. "Well, it appears that was an oversight. Everyone failed to mention that Mr. Franks ordered wine that evening. I understand you took care of him and his dinner companion."

The late-thirties-looking man nodded with a brow cocked and a grin. "Yeah, she was a real looker. Nicely put together."

Bree encouraged him to elaborate, "Tell me more."

"Well, she had a thick, New Yorker-Jersey accent. I know it well. Got relatives from the area. Anyway, well dressed. Dark headed. Stunning looks. The gal had it all. The total package. Probably Italian descent. You know, all hot-blooded and such."

"Why do you use that term?" She squinted toward him.

"We were super busy that night. Everyone wanted wine. So, I spent most of my time running around the room. The gal with Franks got my attention; because, well, she was spectacular. She was angry as hell when she arrived but acted all ladylike and poised. They were battling it out across the table but keeping voices low. First, it was all in whispers. Then as they settled into it, their tones went to normal but heated. After a while, they slowed down; and he did most of the talking. Then it got cozy. Her face softened, and she leaned toward him across the table. He reached across and took her hands in his. It was really sweet the way he played it. You know, the way a gal loves to be treated, all precious and adored."

As he spoke Bree kept taking in big gulps of air. She swallowed a chunk that stuck in her throat. "And when they were finished?"

He shrugged. "Franks held her chair, then put his hand to her back. He kept it there as they left. I never saw either of them again after they walked out of the dining room. My guess is, they had a hot night together. It was clear the two of them were intimate. You know how it is when people have been together. There's a look. You can't miss it."

Clearly, Old Jeff was a romantic paramour and a quality observer of activity in his realm. One had to get their kicks somehow on a job.

"Thank you, Jeffrey. You've been extremely helpful."

"No problem, Ma'am. I hope you catch the killer. It's creepy thinking of him out there running loose."

"No worries. We will get him."

Or her.

She shook Jeff's hand and left.

CHAPTER FIFTEEN

Leaving her car parked in the lot, she stood on the sidewalk in front of the restaurant. If the mystery woman flew in from New York or New Jersey, and if she came to Newport to see Franks, she would likely stay in the closest hotel to his home. Two that fit the bill. One was a block to the right of the restaurant. The other was two blocks to the left.

Bree walked the block to the first. She entered the vast lobby and waited while the hotel desk clerk checked a couple in.

When they walked away, Bree strode to the counter. "I'm hoping you can help me with something." She flipped her ID and pocketed it. "I'm investigating a police case."

"I suppose so. What do you need to know?" The slim, uniformed man smiled graciously.

"I'm looking for a guest who might've stayed here the night of the fifteenth." She showed him the security photo of the woman. "This is her. She might've been from New York or New Jersey."

"I worked the desk that day." He scanned through a computer screen and hit a few buttons. "We had a couple from New York that day, but they were older. Nope. No one stayed here that fits that bill, and I don't recognize the woman."

"Okay, thank you for your help." She turned and left. One more lead checked off her list.

She strolled three blocks to the second facility. Resolve set in. She was in uncharted territory certain the police had not followed this route. Wherever this led, she was going to see it through.

A uniformed man looking to be in his late teens, with short cropped blonde hair manned the front desk of the empty lobby. He looked too young to be working this job, but that wasn't her problem.

He acted up to the role, as he greeted her before she reached his station. "Welcome, how may I serve you?"

She grinned, flipped her wallet identification for him, and stowed it in her pocket. "I'm investigating a police case and have a few questions for you."

"I'm at your service." His chin rose.

"Can you tell me who was on duty the evening of the fifteenth?"

He gave her a broad grin. "That's easy. It was me. I'm on this shift every weekday."

"You may have had a lady guest from the Northeast, likely New York, or New Jersey. This is a photo of the woman." She showed him her phone shot.

His green eyes sparkled. "Oh, yes. I remember her. Nice lady. Very polite." Turning to the computer behind the counter, he clicked a few buttons on the keyboard.

Bree studied the counter. Behind it sat a stack of, what appeared to be, college books and a notepad.

A working student.

That would explain the too-young look. Still, he had to be older than he seemed. He acted like an adult, and it was impressively responsible to work one's way through college. She felt an instant kinship with the young man.

He smiled. "Here she is. She checked in early afternoon on the fifteenth and checked out at four a.m. on the seventeenth."

"Did you see her with a man?"

"No, I noticed her come and go, but never with anyone. She checked in right before I came on duty. Around six-thirty, she left the hotel and returned alone at around nine-thirty. She stopped at the desk and asked for a nine a.m. wake up call for the next day and not to be disturbed until then. I put the wakeup call into the system for her. I wasn't on duty the next morning, but see she got that call from the computer. The next afternoon on the sixteenth, she came in around four p.m. carrying a bunch of shopping bags. Again, she was alone. She called from her room soon after, asking for room service. We were understaffed, so I took her order and gave it to the kitchen staff. She rang the desk about seven and asked about a ride to the airport for the next morning. I booked our shuttle for her for four a.m. on the seventeenth. She asked for a wakeup call at three a.m. and to not be disturbed until then. I put in her orders. I see here, she did check out and took the shuttle as planned. So, I guess she had a flight out."

So, she and Jimmy hadn't spent the night together, as she and Mya figured. "I'm going to need her name and address." She gave him her best stern, business, 'don't bother arguing' look.

He nodded, clicked a few buttons, and printed out the woman's information. Bree folded it and shoved it into her purse. "Thank you for your cooperation and your time."

"No problem. Always happy to help the Authorities." As she left, the man sad down and picked up a thick book.

A giddy stomach accompanied Bree as she strolled from the hotel, not hesitating in case the kid had time to consider and wanted to get a second look at her ID.

"Lord, help me. I'm doing this." Bree spoke to the bright, sunshiny day, as she walked back to her car. "Good thing I brought my credit card."

CHAPTER SIXTEEN

An hour later she stood at the Greater Cincinnati Airport Delta Airline counter. Departing travelers lined up at the baggage check beside her, but she was the only person in this line—a good sign.

A pert, blonde gal in a dark uniform manned the desk. "May I help you?"

"Yes, what is the next flight to La Guardia?" She laid her credit card and driver's license on the countertop.

The woman took them and studied a monitor. "You're in luck. There's one leaving in two hours. It's a direct flight, and two seats are available. One is close to the exit, a middle seat; and one is in the rear near the restrooms."

"I'll take the seat in the back." She groaned to herself when she saw the cost.

The gal rang her charge up, handed the cards back, and the boarding pass to her with a sheet to sign. "Baggage?"

"No, thank you." She picked up the pen attached by a chain to the desktop and signed.

The woman gave no indication her lack of luggage was odd and pointed to Bree's right. "You're set to go. Security is that way. You have just enough time to make it."

Bree strolled to the security line and waited less time than she'd anticipated to be scanned by some sort of radar she hoped didn't outline her thong and cause internal damage to her yet untested reproductive organs. She retrieved her purse after the electronic intrusion and skittered to a tram getting ready to take off into a dark tunnel toward whatever the future brought.

She had just enough time to purchase a pack of gum at a kiosk before settling into an empty seat by the window to watch fellow traveler's bags loaded onto the enormous flying machine. As her behind became comfortable in its chair, a voice on a loudspeaker announced boarding of her flight beginning with those in First and Business Class. She checked her pass for its boarding group. Once a dozen or so elite fliers disappeared through a passageway, the voice called her zone.

She waltzed to the ticketing line. Once she reached the uniformed man admitting passengers at the door, the computer scanner validated her pass, and she walked into the inevitable tunnel. It was a bit like cattle loading into a chute that sent them unbeknownst to their doom. Was she headed for a similar fate by taking this plunge? She shoved the idea to the back of her mind to be delt with while she struggled to fall asleep later that evening, for certain.

After greetings at the entryway by the captain and crew, she took the long walk to the rear where her seat was last before the restrooms and back galley. If the tail of the contraption snapped off in a wreck, she'd be strapped to a flying outhouse. The image sent her into a giggle she had to stifle, so she didn't attract attention of those already boarded. No need to let them know she'd lost her mind.

Which of course, she had. Otherwise, why was she on this solo journey hunting a killer? Without a weapon. Some hunter she was.

After the humongous cavity was loaded with a multitude of willing souls, she did a silent prayer as the roaring engine finally made its way into the air. With eyes closed, she willed a white light to surround her and her compadres in their escapade toward…whatever. She was committed now.

A short flight later, having consumed one toy-sized plastic cup of water, a mini-bag of peanuts, and a couple of dozen thumps on the arm by passersby on their way to use the in-air facilities, the voice announced they were preparing for descent into LaGuardia. The seatbelt sign came on. Passengers were instructed to stow tray tables away, drop trash into the bag being circulated by a steward, and to put seats into the upright position. Of course, hers had remained that way, given it backed up to the wall of the shitter.

Her single visit to the tiny restroom had boosted her respect to anyone who had joined the Mile High Club. If she ever came face-to-face with someone making that claim, she intended to insist on details as to how exactly it was done. She had failed to purchase a book for the flight, so had spent more than enough in-air down time mulling it over. Still, she could not figure out a way.

LaGuardia was alive and kicking when she disembarked, though it had taken more time than she'd thought possible to land, taxi, and unload the giant aircraft. Big was big, but damn, who had thought there'd be a traffic jam of airplanes waiting for taxi rights. It was worse than Sunday morning back home trying to get out of the church parking lot.

She strolled among the people brave enough to travel in and out of this vast city, following signage toward Baggage Claim. Surely that would send her in the right direction.

A moving sidewalk, a long jaunt, a tram ride, another lengthy walk, a second tram, and a short walk, finally, she arrived at the enormous sea of luggage conveyances. Center most, gratefully, she strode to an information booth. The smiling attendant behind the desk, in an unidentified uniform, greeted her at eight-thirty p.m. Already, it had been a long day.

"Thank you. Is there an airport hotel where I could get a room for the night?" Bree gave her most pleasing smile.

"Of course, ma'am." The pretty girl pointed to a far wall of phones. "There are more than twelve hotels in or around the airport. The three on the left are the closest. You might try those first."

"Thank you." Bree turned and walked to the wall. A backlit visual displayed the facility above each phone. She picked up the first receiver, asked for a room for the night. The informant advised her they were fully booked. The second was the same. The third receiver's voice told her they had two available, a suite and a single with a king-sized bed.

"I'll take that one." She gave her credit card number and personal identification information to the voice, who provided a confirmation number and instructions on how to find the shuttle to her bed. Bree could hardly wait.

Exiting the doors as told, she walked across four lanes of traffic to an island marked "Hotel Shuttles." Finding the name she sought, she stood in line beneath the sign, along with a half a dozen others. No one seemed to notice her lack of baggage.

A ten-minute wait and half an hour drive, she stepped out and strolled into the well-lit, no-nonscience facility. It appeared clean and efficient. Soon she was issued a key card, and upon request, a gift bag filled with a toothbrush, a tiny tube of toothpaste, mini bottles of lotion, shampoo, conditioner, and a cotton pair of footies. "Is there someplace I can purchase food without having to go far?"

The pleasant night clerk shrugged. You can take a cab to the Denny's across the street, but it's a hazardous walk. We have vending." He opened the door to a cubbyhole beside his countertop desk, revealing a wall of food and drink machines and a rack of New York souvenir shirts.

She smiled and stepped inside the cubbyhole, no larger than a walk-in closet. Selecting a chicken salad sandwich, bag of chips, and drink from vending machines, she turned and picked out a shirt that looked like it would more than fit her. She paid the man for the tee shirt and took the bank of elevators to her floor.

Settled into the economy-sized room with its giant bed, she stripped and pulled the big 'I Heart NY' shirt on, peeled cellophane from the sandwich, and opened her chips and water. She drew out her phone and hit SEND on the automatic dial icon.

Time to face the music.

Mya's voice sounded tense. "Bree, are you on your way home? I'm pulling a meatloaf out of the oven now."

Bree sniffed her convenience meal. Aroma of homecooked meatloaf failed to tantalize her nostrils, making her regret once again her decision to do the most ridiculous thing ever.

"No, sorry, Mya. I got caught up in investigating the dark-haired woman lead. I'm actually at a hotel in New York City. I found the woman, and I'm going to go see her tomorrow morning."

A gush of air from Mya's surprise did more than vibrate Bree's ear. It made her feel guilty...guilty for worrying her dear aunt.

"Bree, what on earth? What were you thinking? Get yourself home. Now. Well. Maybe wait until tomorrow morning. Have a good night's sleep. You undoubtedly paid for the room. Then come home soon as you get up. Heaven's sake, Bree, you can't be galivanting all over the country playing detective. Let the police handle this."

A voice of reason overtook Bree's less positive inner being as she listened to her aunt spout her frustration. Solemn confidence slipped over her. "Mya, I hear you. Seriously, I understand your concern. It's going to be fine. I know who this woman is, and I aim to meet her before returning home. It will be okay. From what I learned, she and Jimmy ended their time together in Newport on a genial note. There was clearly a close relationship between them, but I do not believe she is his killer. She may be involved in some way, but I can't see her doing that to him. I need to better understand how she's involved, to find out if it has anything at all to do with his death."

"Bree, please come home. Don't do this. Call Rex and let him handle it."

Bree sighed heavily. Rex would scold her for taking action of any kind, especially this. Guilt at hiding what she was up to from him was smothered by freshly sprouted confidence. She'd already gotten farther than his people had on this lead. She needed to see it through. Her life and that of her precious aunt were Bree's responsibility. She wasn't about to entrust Mya's future to the police now.

"I'm sorry, Mya. I promise to be extremely careful, but I am doing this." A wave of calm enveloped her, and she knew she would be fine...no matter what happened.

"Call me tomorrow." Mya knew Bree better than anyone and must've heard her resolve.

CHAPTER SEVENTEEN

Bree partook of the complimentary breakfast, unsure when she'd obtain nourishment again, and boarded the hotel shuttle to the train station for the twenty-minute drive. Finding a train that would take her to downtown, she bought a ticket and climbed onboard. The tram car smelled like a strange combination of urine and bleach. She chose a seat without bubblegum visibly attached and settled into the barely ripped vinyl upholstery for the lengthy, bumpy, railcar ride. She followed lead of other passengers and tried not to meet anyone's eyes. Feeling like a bear in a swarm of irate bees, she clutched her purse against her belly as they zoomed into the long, dark tunnel.

Finally, disembarking at Grand Central Station, Bree was in awe of its grand appearance, appearing to be the center of the New York City universe. Hundreds of people scurried in every direction, acting as though this was nothing out of the ordinary.

Talk about a little fish in a big pond.

There must have been more people in this one building than inhabited her whole hometown.

A bit overwhelmed, she sought calm by taking charge and located an information booth. A grizzled, middle-aged man looked up from his paper, grumbled something in the way of directions, and tossed a street guide at her.

"Thanks." She turned away and studied the map, trying to make sense of his sparse, curt words, and thick accent with which she was unfamiliar.

She left the massive structure and made her way along a densely populated street. Everyone she encountered, and there were hundreds of them, seemed to be going in the opposite direction. Two blocks later and across the busy street, she spotted the sign she was seeking. Taking her life in her hand, she went with the flow as the WALK sign lit green, staying mid-crowd so she wouldn't be the first to be plowed into by some cabbie in a hurry.

After a fifteen-minute wait, she boarded the double-decker, red bus and climbed steps to the top layer. Taking a seat, her head scanned around.

Buildings in Cincinnati were nothing compared to these. Even the tallest of them was about the size of a short New York skyscraper. She gawked at random, obviously in the company of other tourists. A Japanese family with a bunch of teenagers snapped continual photographs.

New York really was the Big Apple. She might've enjoyed its draw if she had come on anything other than a murder hunt. It might be nice to visit with Mya, do some shopping in fabulous stores they passed, tour the many museums and historical attractions, and go to plays in the Theatre District. There was so much to see, and she'd only gotten a short glimpse of the Statue of Liberty and Ellis Island during landing.

The darned bus stopped every few blocks, so the ride took forever, winding its way through village after village, until it stopped at the location she'd marked on her map, Soho. She climbed down and off the bus, stowing her ticket in her blazer pocket. The all-day pass gave her the right to get on and off at any stop she chose. She intended to make her way to the airport by backtracking the way she'd come.

She took a minute to get her bearings then strolled into the corner drug store and purchased a bottle of water, a couple granola bars, and a pack of cheese crackers. Living in a rural area her whole life, she'd learned it paid to be prepared.

Hiking the three blocks east her map showed she needed to take, she eyed the eclectic buildings. Mostly aged and worn by weather, they were largely constructed of huge blocks of rock or formed concrete. Most were several stories tall, thin, and had steps up to the first floors. Windows aligned with the sidewalk and steps downward indicated lower-level apartments. Steps directly met the sidewalk, with no visible grass to be seen. An occasional shade tree sprouted from squares of dirt near the curbs, along with various newspaper vending machines, metal trash cans chained inside strips of steel surrounding them, and every so often a fire hydrant. She was completely out of her element here.

Eventually, her stroll led to the address she was looking for. The paper in her purse confirmed it was the location. She mounted the six stone steps between two elaborately formed concrete railings to a landing in front of a wide, antique wooden door. A panel of buzzers was lined one side, each with a name above it. Fourth down the tab read 'L. Alessandra.' This had to be her mystery woman.

Bree pushed the buzzer and waited. No answer.

She pushed again. The same.

Waiting a couple of minutes, she gazed around. Two sturdy pots on the top of the wide handrail housed a splash of colorful flowers in a variety of colors. It appeared at odds with the starkness of the buildings. Someone here had a green thumb. Lovely contrast of the flowers against their neighboring backdrop felt sad. The poor things must feel lonely, maybe even terrified in their surroundings; but they were thriving—like Bree.

She was on a roll and feeling proud to have plopped herself into such a strange world, having successfully achieved what she could so far of her goal. Her shoulders rocked back, and she tapped the button again.

No answer.

A glance at her phone told her it wasn't wise to find something productive or entertaining to do while waiting. She might as well stick it out. She'd come this far. No leaving without getting what she came for.

She hopped her behind up onto the thick stone rail and cracked open her water bottle. After a swig, she put the container into her bag and watched what little activity was happening around her in the late morning. Most people were probably sleeping off the night shift or had gone to work or school by now. Not many were milling around.

Could she live in such close proximity to the masses? Anything was possible, but she had no desire to find out. Greater Cincinnati was as populated an area as she was interested in. It had taken a divorce and losing her only other living relative to entice Bree to leave her sleepy, rural hometown for Newport, Kentucky.

An hour later, she spied her target. The dark-haired woman rounded a far corner dressed in a classic skirt-and-jacket suit and wearing short heels to match. Her hair and makeup were done to perfection.

She was being pulled by a tiny dog at the end of a leash, meandering from post-to-tree-to-any upright structure between the corner and their destination. The woman must've had all the time in the world. She gave the little pug every opportunity he sought out to mark his territory and sniff out danger.

When they finally arrived at the brownstone, the gal dropped a tied plastic bag she'd been carrying into a trash receptacle at the curb, stooped, and scooped up the little pug. She turned and took the stairs up with a lilt in her step, never catching Bree's gaze or acknowledging her presence. She pulled out a key.

Before the mystery lady could shove it into the keyhole, Bree hopped down. "Ms. Alessandra?"

The gal turned, eyed Breed up and down without changing expressions. "Yes."

Bree heard a quiver in her own voice. "Ma'am, I'm Bree Collins, and I'd like to ask you some questions."

The woman's face went to stone. "I'm sorry. I don't give interviews." She spun, showing Bree her backside, and attempted to insert her key.

"Ms. Alessandra, Lola Alessandra? I didn't come for an interview, but I would like to talk with you."

"No, I'm sorry. I'm very busy." The fob plunged into the keyhole."

Fear she'd wasted her trip sent adrenaline through Bree's veins and bolstered her courage. "I've come a long way to talk with you . . . from Newport, Kentucky. I need your help. I'm here about James Franks."

The brunette's head whipped around without turning her body. She glared." After a second, she worked the doorknob and flung the door wide. Stepping inside, she strode toward a bank of stairs. Bree caught the closing door.

A stern voice shot over Mystery Lady's shoulder. "You coming?" She didn't slow down, but fast walked up a flight of stairs. Bree caught up with her as she raced down a short hallway to a door at the end.

Bree was breathing hard when the gal inserted keys in three locks and clicked them open. She pushed the door wide, sat the dog down, and removed his leash. Hanging it on a hook by the door with her purse, she waited for Bree to follow her inside then flipped the three keyed locks sound, slid a dead bolt closed, and pulled a chain lock into place.

Bree had never been so securely sealed away from the rest of the world. Hell, back home people rarely even locked their doors.

Without a word, the strange female strode to the kitchen area behind a bar with two stool-height chairs in the large great room area. As Bree followed, the gal flipped an overhead cabinet open and pulled out a bottle of amble liquid.

She bent and pulled a container from a bottom cabinet, filled the dog's bowl with kibble, and replaced the carton. The little guy quickly began gobbling it down.

From a second cabinet, she chose two short tumblers and strutted to a two-person table along a wall. She sat her items down and poured a couple thumbs of bourbon into one glass and took one of the two seats.

Glancing up, she met Bree's eyes. "Join me?"

Bree sat across from her with a nod. Her host poured a second helping of liquor and shoved it to her guest. Ms. Alessandra swigged down the drink in one gulp, closed her eyes and inhaled deeply then poured herself another.

The small dog finished his meal and strolled to his master's side, lying down and placing his ruffled face on her foot as a pillow. His eyes closed, and he appeared to doze off.

Bree took a sip. Good Kentucky bourbon was a delightful treat. It wouldn't hurt to allow it to help build her courage and squash remaining qualms about sitting locked away from eyes of the public with this strange woman who could be a killer.

Room-temperature fire blazed a path across her tongue, deliciously coating it and leaving the urge for more before descending along her throat and igniting a sting that sizzled all the way to her now-empty stomach. Her eyes closed to relish her body's reaction to intense character of the malted beverage.

One had to appreciate quality of good liquor.

Her gaze opened to the woman's stare. "You're from Kentucky?"

"Yes, how did you know?" Bree frowned.

Lola Alessandra's dark brow cocked. "For starters, you have an accent; and you called him James Franks."

Funny. She'd thought Lola the one with an accent. "Why is that strange?"

"Well, his name is Frank C. James, not James Franks. Franklin Cydrick James."

Bree's mind did a twist-turn. "Wow, that's odd. You and Frank James were close?"

Why would he use a fake name? It didn't make sense.

Lola nodded. "Yes, very. We lived together for four years, though we'd known each other since we were kids."

Bree closed her eyes and winced. *She must have loved Jimmy, no, Frank.* Pity for Ms. Alessandra filtered in and pushed out Bree's anxiety about asking questions. There was something to learn here—important information. Her determination grew.

Bree put a hand between them on the small table. "Are you aware of his death?"

Lola sighed heavily, as her shoulders fell; and she stared at the ceiling, blinking. "No, but it doesn't surprise me. How did it happen?" Her tearful eyes met Bree's.

What to reveal? Her heart told her everything. Her brain screamed she was being a fool. *Take it slow.* "He scummed to heart failure."

Lola's large, dark eyes grew wider. "No, not Frankie. That can't be. He was healthy and strong when I saw him only last week. He had no history of heart problems, and no one in his family did either."

Bree hadn't thought of that. Someone needed to be notified—a next of kin. "You know his family?"

The dark head's shake jiggled curls around Lola's shoulders. "No. Frankie was an only child. His parents came over together from Italy when they married and died while we were in college. Their folks were killed during World War II."

Like Bree's Dad. Sympathy filtered her words. "So, you're the closest thing he had to family? James doesn't sound Italian."

Lola blinked a couple times. "I guess I am. Yes, it's not. Frankie's parents shortened their name from Jamettelli to James, Americanized it. When last we talked, Frankie told me he'd found someone else to love. He was happy to see me in one way but sorry in another. He said my finding him meant others could too, and he would have to leave his Mya behind."

So, he did love Mya.

At least, Bree could bring her that information. It might help sooth her aunt's broken heart. Bree leaned forward, elbows on the table. "I don't understand."

Lola got up and fished a small album from a credenza. "This is Frankie and me." She pointed to one of several photographs of her and James together. They looked the adoring couple."

"We were incredibly happy together, at least I thought so. I believed we would be together forever. I was naive back then. Never questioned anything Frankie said or did. Looking back, I should have." Lola's well-manicured finger stroked the photos.

Bree simpered. "I can definitely relate, divorced myself." Many times, Bree should've questioned

Oran's actions or words. "Hindsight is twenty-twenty, as they say."

Lola swigged her jigger of whiskey. "Ain't it a bitch?"

Bree began to relax, rather liking this, Lola. "Indeed, it is." Either the bourbon was doing the trick, or it was the reaction of the strange woman with whom she was drinking. Probably a little of both.

Lola poured another tumbler for herself. "Speaking of bitches, do you believe in Karma?"

Bree nursed her own in hand on the table. "I do. Why?"

"When Frankie met me for dinner in Newport, I told him I believe in it. He did a lot of bad things, hurt a lot of people. His karma didn't look good. I guess, it came back to bite him. I never figured he'd go out peacefully with a heart attack, though."

Bree winced. "He didn't exactly die in his sleep. He succumbed to heart failure as a result of torture. Someone cut his fingertips off. We don't know who or why. I am hoping you can tell me something that will help lead the police to his killer. It's why I've come."

A sad nod answered. "That's more what I expected. Poor son of a bitch, I hate to think of it; but it doesn't surprise me."

Bree gripped her glass. "Why is that?"

"Frankie hurt a lot of people. Wrecked families. He stole life savings from lots of folks. They're bitter. Can't say they don't have a right to be. They've taken it out on me for a long time. Before he disappeared with all that cash, Frankie and I lived in Jersey above my family store. After he left, I got death threats, nasty letters, you name it, for a couple years. People egged and threw tomatoes at my store windows. A guy lobbed a wine bottle inside and hit one of my cashiers. Poor thing had a concussion. One son-of-a-bitch broke into my home while I was out and tore the place up but didn't steal anything. It was awful."

Bree gushed. "They held you responsible?"

Lola winced. "Of course, they did. For a long time, the Feds believed I was in on it with Frankie. Maybe still do. They tailed me everywhere. I don't know if they thought Frankie would contact me, if I'd eventually lead them to him, or if I'd finally show my hand and start spending my share of the take. They must've finally given up on me. I don't catch them shadowing me anymore, or maybe I'm just used to it. The Feds were one thing, but people are different. They never gave up. Even those I considered close friends turned against me. I finally had to sell my store for much less than it was worth. I moved here to the city, bought a small coffee shop a couple blocks away and this brownstone apartment. I keep to myself, a loner. Don't think my neighbors know who I am. You know, New Yorkers usually protect their privacy. It's a defense, I guess."

Bree's heart wanted to comfort the woman who had endured so much pain on Frank James' account, but the more she learned the more she needed answers. Bree and Mya had their own problems he had caused. "So, how did you find Frankie?"

Mya grimaced and took another swig of the strong brew. "I was having another one of those nights when I couldn't sleep, watching late night television. The anchor was doing a show on heroes across the land. They did a clip on a Newport, Kentucky man who rescued his next-door neighbor from a home fire. It barely got my attention until the cloudy visual of Frankie carrying some old woman out of a blazing house came on the screen. I recognized him instantly, just from the way he moved and that gorgeous face of his. Then they showed a clearer video of him, the old gal, and a pretty woman about my age standing in front of another house. Frankie and the one he'd saved had towels around their necks, and the women were dressed in night clothes."

"The other woman was Mya—the pretty one your age." It couldn't do any harm telling her that. She acted fine with Frankie finding a new love.

Lola's winced. "I'm sorry to have caused her grief. Even if he hadn't died, she would've lost him on my account. He said he had to leave her, for the same reason he left me behind. Neither of us was suited for a life of running and hiding, a life of crime."

Bree nodded. "For certain, Mya isn't. She would never have condoned what he had done."

"Neither did I, but I forgave him for leaving me behind. He did it for my own good. He couldn't resist stealing that money. He handled so much of it at work. It got the better of him. Greed, you know? Sad, and I'll never understand it; but I did forgive him. Pitiful, when you think of it. He and I made enough working. We could've eventually been fairly wealthy, had we saved and invested wisely. Frankie said he couldn't wait—not with all that cash flowing through his fingers every day. Leaving me alone and in the dark was the best thing he could do for me, under the circumstances. He couldn't do that to Mya either. He knew she'd never forgive what he'd done."

Bree gave her a sad nod. "How exactly did he embezzle all that money?"

Lola sucked in a deep breath, and her shoulders rose and fell. "The FBI told me he created a fake investment holding he only shared with his targets. Everything about it appeared on the up and up. He faked everything from the NASDAC number to history of growth and legal documentation to back it all up. He sold them shares in the bogus stock and pocketed the money. Apparently, he intended to let them down with bad news the stock had tanked at some point in the future—when he'd taken them for enough cash to satisfy his greed." Tears welled in Lola's eyes as she spoke, and she blinked but didn't wipe them away. "Frankie must've gotten wind the SEC and FBI were about to raid him, because he just up and disappeared without a trace."

Bree frowned, her heart breaking for the beautiful, emotional woman. "That's so sad."

Lola grimaced. "At least I got closure from our meeting. I never figured to hear from him again. I hate thinking I might have led the killer to him. I could be responsible for his death." Lola wiped tears from her cheeks with a paper napkin.

Bree's hand shot across the table and covered Lola's against the glass she held. "Don't even go there. If his death has anything to do with the theft, it is not your doings. He made his own bed, his own choices. They have nothing to do with you. If they're related to that debacle, the killer could just as easily have seen that news clip as you did. It's not your fault. There's nothing to prove Frankie's death had anything to do with his theft anyway. Frankie wasn't liked by everyone he met. The man had made new enemies during the last five years." Bree's mind wondered to the day she had overheard the argument at the County Clerk's Office.

Lola looked up. "You came to check me out. Didn't you? You thought I killed Frankie."

Bree shrugged and took a sip of her liquor. "I had to know."

Lola's head rocked to the side. "And?"

Bree smiled with a closed mouth. "And I don't believe you had anything to do with it. I'm happy to feel that way, but mostly glad to give you the information before you hear it on television or from the FBI. I'm also happy to be able to tell Mya Frankie loved her." She stood to leave then recalled something else. "The money hasn't been recovered. They have found no trace of his cash or computer. How much did Frankie steal?"

Lola met her eyes. "A little over five-million dollars." She looked away and appeared to consider that for a few seconds. Bree stood silently, hoping to find something that might spur the police in the right direction. "Let me show you something."

She hopped up and strode to a credenza against a wall. Bree took her seat again, and Lola returned with a manila envelope. She opened it and pulled out a thick stack of papers with a few photographs on top.

Laying one on the table, she pointed. "Frankie was always paranoid about security. He never left his computer out, not even to go to the restroom. It was either always at his side, or it was locked away in the trunk of his car or our safe."

Bree frowned. "That looks like a television hanging on the wall." What she saw didn't jive with what Lola said.

Lola flipped it aside to reveal the next photo. "Oh, it is . That's the TV in our apartment in Jersey."

It was beginning to make more sense.

Lola sniffed as she flipped to another. "This shot shows how it moves aside. Frankie installed a button under a windowsill that wasn't clearly visible. When you pushed the button, the TV moved to reveal the cubicle he installed. He stowed his computer here." She pointed to a slim compartment about five inches wide and about thirty inches tall. "Now I look back at things, I guess he kept the stolen money in this safe. Frankie said he didn't trust banks, so he needed a safe. I never questioned him about it at the time."

"And you never opened the safe?" Bree's head tilted, and her brows furrowed.

Lola shrugged. "No, why would I? I never used it, didn't have jewelry worth locking up. I kept my savings in a bank. I had no idea the man I loved would do such a thing. I trusted him."

It was easy to see how that might be true. Bree had been much the same with Oran for many a year.

Lola revealed a shot of the empty vault with its door opened. "I had no idea, until the FBI showed up with warrants for damned near everything. I opened the safe for them, but it was too late. Empty."

Bree's left brow shot up. "You had the combination?"

Lola sneered. "Sadly, yes. Frankie was awful at remembering numbers. He never changed his passwords. It was five, nineteen, nineteen-fifty-nine for as long as I could remember. It was the safe combination, and I suppose it is still his computer combo—if you're able to locate it. It's his birthday."

Bree pulled her phone out and made a note of the number. "Okay if I take photos of these visuals?"

Lola snickered. "Sure, no problem." She laid the four photographs out in a square so Bree could get them all into one shot. "The FBI has copies, too."

What else might Rex want?

Bree bit her lower lip. Moving the photos revealed photocopies of handwritten notes. "Are those the threats you received?"

Lola nodded, sides of her mouth dropping. "Yes, the Feds made copies for me when they took the originals. You know, just in case." Her eyes closed briefly with a sigh.

How could she get copies of them? "You know what would really be helpful is a list of the victims of Frankie's scheme. I suppose the police can request that from the FBI."

Lola patted the stack of paper in front of her. "No need. I have a list of the names and their contact information. The FBI said I might need to share it with the police, should something happen to me as a result of Frankie's actions. I can make you a set." She picked the papers up and walked to a small secretary desk across the room. Flipping it up, a small desktop printer came into view. The pub scampered to his mistress' side as she put the stack into a section of the device and hit a button. "I'll copy the notes as well. One never knows who might be involved."

Bree was more and more certain this woman had nothing to do with Frank C. James' death. She was being more than compliant. "That would be wonderful. You know I'll have to share what you've told with the Newport Police Department."

Lola's head nodded, as she continued working the printer. "Not a problem. I'm used to being interrogated, but it's been a while. I'll write my cell phone number on the back of the first page. Tell them to call me. I'm available to help any way I can, and they may not want to fly all the way to New York like you did."

Bree snickered. "You're right, but I'm glad I did." In any other situation, she could see herself, Mya and Lola becoming friends. At least they weren't enemies.

Lola met her eyes across the room. "I am too. Something about your visit has changed me. Between talking with you and my visit with Frankie, I feel freer than I have in years. It's like a ball and chain have been removed from around me." She picked up the two stacks of paper and brought them back to the table with a manilla envelope.

Freedom was doubtful to be long lived. "You realize once the press learns James Frank's true identity, they'll put two-and-two together. There's going to be a firestorm of publicity not only in Northern Kentucky, but here in New York as well."

Lola sat down and slid her set back into their place. She put the fresh copies into the clean envelope. "I know. It's going to get rough around here again. My neighbors are going to figure out who I really am." She sighed. "My parents moved to Florida when they retired, and I took over the grocery. I'm not so hot on that area. Other than a couple trips to visit them and the jaunt to locate Frankie in Newport, I've never been anywhere other than New York. I might just put my coffee shop and this apartment on the market and do a little exploring. I've always wanted to see Arizona, the Grand

Canyon, and Sedona. I might check it out, Montana and Wyoming, too. Maybe even Alaska. What do you think?" She smiled, a bit sadly.

Bree smiled conspiratorially. "I hear Hawaii is fabulous."

Lola nodded. "Yeah, that too. A little walk-about might just be the ticket to finding a fresh start where no one knows or cares about what my past lover did." She handed the envelope to Bree.

Bree stashed it in her purse and stood. "I'd best be going. Don't want to impose more than I already have. I'm happy you're doing okay and not involved in Frankie's killing."

Lola and the pug followed Bree to the door. The woman picked the little guy up and snuggled him, rubbing her chin on his wrinkled face. "Cyd here and I are glad you came. He's been my only real company for the last four years. I can't recall when I last sat and just talked with a live human—except for that visit with Frankie." Her mouth drooped, and tears flowed once more but were ignored.

The dog was named after Frankie—middle name Cydric. *Funny.*

Lola unlocked the five contraptions securing her personal space. "It was good meeting you, Bree. You're always welcome here—or wherever I land."

Bree offered her hand and shook the warm, satiny one her host offered. "I wish you the best." She handed Lola a Pampered Tigress business card with her name and phone number on it. "Stay in touch. Let me know where you end up."

"Thank you, Bree." The door locks clicked into place behind Bree as she took the stairs toward the exit.

Hopefully, Lola Alessandra would find a fresh start somewhere she doesn't have to imprison herself behind five security locks.

CHAPTER EIGHTEEN

Bree took the multi-mode trip back to the airport
and called the airline while in transit. She booked a
return flight for early evening but wasn't lucky
enough to get a non-stop flight. Finally, boarded and
cramped between two chubby passengers crowding
her armrests on both sides, she endured the two-hour
flight to Cleveland. Luckily, her seat companions got
off.

While new passengers were boarding, she took
the aisle seat with hopes she wouldn't be outed. With
luck, she only had one flight companion for the
remainder of the jaunt to Greater Cincinnati Airport.
The plane barely had time to go up to flight level
before it began descent into the airport. Dusk was
starting to set over the horizon, and she was
exhausted.

The airport was nearly deserted when she disembarked and strolled through the terminal to the tram that took her to the baggage claim area. Exiting, she found the shuttle to her parking lot; and in a few minutes, she headed East on I275. Forty-five minutes later, she took the exit ramp to Newport and the ten-minute cruise home.

Pulling into the driveway, she hit the garage door opener. In the rearview mirror two blue-uniformed men left the empty burnout lot on the corner across the street and jumped into a dark grey sedan. The car pulled away as the garage door shut. Mya's car was in the garage, so her aunt was home.

Bree trudged into the kitchen, tossed her handbag onto the counter beside where Mya sat nursing a goblet of wine. Her arms opened, and Bree fell into them.

"I'm so glad you're home. You look exhausted."

"That's for sure." Bree drew away and rounded the counter.

"There's meatloaf. I figured you'd be hungry, so I made you a plate."

Bree pulled out the plastic covered dish. "Thanks. I'm starved." She put it in the microwave then reached for the half empty bottle. Tilting it and her heads, her aunt nodded in answer. Bree topped off Mya's glass, then got one for herself from an overhead cabinet. She poured the rest into it, then plopped the empty into the trash. The beeper sounded. She retrieved her food and took it to sit beside her aunt.

Sipping her wine, she closed her eyes and took a deep breath then exhaled. "Thanks for this. I appreciate it."

Mya patted her hand. "Of course, it's the least I could do. You've literally gone way past what you told me you were going to do and put your life on the line for me. Whatever you need, I'm here."

Bree began to eat and between bites, explained how she'd identified the dark-haired woman.

Mya sighed. "Why didn't the police learn this? I'm sure they would've followed up on it, and why didn't you just go to Rex with what you learned, like you said you would do."

Bree winced then ignored the last question. "They talked to the same people I did at first, but I went further and asked if there might be someone else in the restaurant that evening, who could've seen a bit more. I found the sommelier spent a great deal of time in the room. He was observant and extremely helpful. What I learned from him, led me to check area hotels with her description, the photo from the restaurant's security system, and a broad idea of where the Mystery Lady might've come from. I hit gold when I spoke with the desk clerk at the third hotel. He recognized her and pulled up her name and address for me."

"Why would he give you that information?" Mya's brows furrowed.

Bree cringed. "Well, he might've gotten the impression I was working with the police department. I didn't correct his assumption. It's not a complete lie of omission. Soon as I finish eating, I'll call Rex and fill him in. Guess what else I learned."

Mya shook her head, eyes to the ceiling. "I should've known you wouldn't just hand it over and let the police do the dirty work." She picked up her goblet and eased back into the counter-height seat. "So, what did you learn?"

"I went to visit the woman. Her name is Lola Alessandra, and she lives in SoHo, New York. She wasn't home when I arrived, but she showed up an hour later. She thought I was with the press and didn't want to talk with me. I refused to leave. When I dropped the name James Franks, she immediately opened the door and took me to her apartment. She didn't speak again until we were seated at a table with a bottle of bourbon." She was aware of heightening aura of suspense building as she spoke.

Mya frowned. "Why would she think you were the press?"

"Apparently, she has been hounded by them for years since Jimmy disappeared. She was his lover, and they lived together. They knew each other their whole lives. She was shocked when she found out what he was doing and why he suddenly disappeared. Poor thing had to learn it from the Feds."

"I don't understand." Mya sat her wine down and stared.

"James Franks is an alias. His name is Franklin Cydric James. He was a stockbroker for a New York firm, and he embezzled over five-million dollars from his clients. Somehow, he must've got word the SEC and FBI were about to nab him, took the cash and disappeared without a trace. They have been looking for him for years. At first the FBI thought Lola was in on it, and he'd contact her, or she'd lead them to James. Over the years, they have cleared her, but the public and media continued to harass the poor woman. James ruined her business and life, but she had loved him."

Mya's head cocked, and her chin scrunched up into a pouting expression. "You sound awful chummy with this Lola person."

Bree bit her lower lip. "I do like her. She's a decent person; and like you, Jimmy did her wrong. Under different circumstances, you'd like her also." She paused watching as Mya absorbed this information with a pensive look.

Mya frowned. "I don't get it. How did she find him when the FBI couldn't?"

Bree sighed. "Lola saw a late-night broadcast of James saving your neighbor. She knew him better than anyone and recognized him immediately. It didn't take much research for her to track him down from that. Surely, the Feds would've found him soon, had she not. That kind of thing always gets back to them."

Mya nodded, her lips turned down and eyes shaded. "I'm sure they would. If they haven't already gotten wise, Rex will alert them soon as you tell him about Jimmy. What a fool I am. I was duped by a slick-talking, handsome man. I was in love with him, or who I thought he was. None of it was real. I'm such an idiot."

Bree's hand flew to rest on Mya's forearm. "No, Mya, you're not; and it was real. Lola said when she contacted him and he met her for dinner, he told her everything. Frank confessed he'd let his greed take control and couldn't resist all that money running through his fingers every day. He loved her enough to leave her behind. Had he even said goodbye, it would've put her in jeopardy. Leaving her was the only solution to protect her. It kept her out of jail but still ruined her life. Her business failed. People were horrible to her. She received threats on her life, and they continually tormented her everywhere she went. She moved and lives basically in isolation." Bree stopped for a breather.

"What's that got to do with me and Jimmy?" Mya's brows wrinkled.

"When they talked, James said he'd finally settled into a new life and found someone to love. He told her about you, even your name. He admitted he was in love with you." She paused, watching strain around Mya's eyes soften. "Lola's really a nice woman, and under other circumstances we might all be friends. Confronting James gave her a new lease on life. The press will be hot on her trail again, but she's going to move somewhere no one knows her. She's free after all these years. Lola wanted you to know James loved you."

Mya's lower lip curled up. "Too bad for Jimmy. Giving her closure might be the reason he's dead."

Bree nodded. "Could be. Maybe not. There are others he's made enemies of right here in Newport. I'm sure Rex and his people will soon figure out who did this." Hopefully she was right and not just painting sunny skies and rainbows for Mya when a downpour was about to crash down and flood their lives.

"Yes, and you need to call Rex so he can get on that as soon as possible." Mya took her goblet to the dishwasher. "I'm exhausted."

Bree loaded her own dishes inside it also. "I'll do that before I go up for the night." She gave Mya a peck on the cheek. "As a matter of fact, I have a good idea where James might've hidden his computer and money."

Mya smiled. "Wonderful, but it's too late to pursue it tonight."

Bree took her seat. "Yes, I'll invite Rex over for coffee tomorrow."

Mya waved a hand. "Good. See you in the morning." She strolled from the kitchen as Bree hit speed dial.

Rex's smooth, strong tenor always made her smile. "Hello, Sunshine. Where have you been? I've tried calling you several times today."

Her nose curled. "I noticed. Sorry about that. I forgot to charge my phone and let the battery run down. Was it important?"

Confidence she admired in the man painted his words. "Might be. Not sure yet, but it certainly is interesting. I know how concerned you are about Mya and you being on my murder board. I just wanted to let you know, you're not the only photos up there. Since you pointed me in that direction, I owe you the courtesy of an update on our Planning and Zoning Commissioner."

Her heart lurched with promise. "You found something on Jefferson Rose?"

"We've talked with him, his wife Harriet Burns-Rose, the Mayor, County Clerk Candy Palmer, and some other people who work in the courthouse and learned enough to get a subpoena for Rose's financial records. Turns out he has been living the high life. His mansion has a small mortgage, but nothing near what it's worth—the property is valued at a great deal more than his salary should afford. We found he had used inside information to purchase several key plots of land near areas getting ready for expansion."

"Isn't that illegal?" Eagerness revealed itself in her voice. Should she be more discreet?

Nah. She wanted to level with Rex. Otherwise, they had no chance for a future relationship—assuming this damned murder got solved.

She imagined him screwing his mouth up adorably, causing the cleft in his chin to show. "One would think so, but not in his position, though it is unethical. If he was selling stocks or bonds, yes. It would be."

He was getting uncomfortably close to what she had to tell him. "What does that mean?"

"Nothing by itself. Combine that with the sales being for cash—cash we couldn't find a money trail for. It led us to believe he might be doing exactly what you said. We've questioned several large developers of local properties who obtained permits over the last few years and discovered he has been bilking kickbacks from them for providing timely permits. These cases are going to be investigated to ensure permits were not issued where they should not have been."

"What about James' permit? I understand it was confirmed the day he was killed."

Please, let this lead to the killer.

Her silent prayer was in Rex's capable, tender but powerful hands. "Commissioner Rose isn't as slick at hiding money as James Franks was. There was a large deposit of cash in his bank account the day before he signed Franks' permit. We believe it came from Franks."

She took a satisfying inhale. "I could tell those two hated each other. Bitterness followed them like a cloud that day I overheard them arguing, as they plowed out of Rose's office."

"When Franks first came to town, he hired Attorney Anson Butler to handle the purchase of his first plot of development land—the parcel where the subdivision he, you, and Mya live on now. Butler remained his lawyer and created all the vendor and sales contracts, deed to the new lots, and anything else Franks needed legal advice for. He worked on the purchase of the new development as well. As it turns out, Franks put a very minute down payment toward an option to buy, contingent on his securing permits, and the balance of the sales price not payable until he completed development, construction, and as each house sold. He never actually bought that land."

She grimaced and stuttered, "What…what…does that have to do with Rose?"

Rex's exhale came through the phone. "It wasn't just business between Rose and Franks. There's a personal vendetta between them. Harriet Burns worked for Butler as a paralegal. She was single at the time and worked closely with Franks on his first project. They started seeing each other outside of work. Evidently, she was also dating Rose at the time. Franks apparently knew about Rose, but Rose didn't know about him. Or he was bitter about her playing the field with Franks. Rose was extremely jealous. The mayor told me he attended Butler's Christmas party that first year Franks was in town. Franks was there when Harriet showed up with her date, Commissioner Rose. Rose confronted Franks in the dining room, and a pushing shouting match ensued. Before punches could fly and a complete row destroyed his party, Butler broke the men up and told Harriet to take her date home so he could cool off."

"Wow, so the real hot head was Rose, not necessarily Franks." She might've misjudged Frank James.

"It sounds that way. James acted with courtesy and class when I was around him. The Mayor, Butler, and Harriet attested to the same thing. Harriet and Rose were married the spring after the holiday party skuttle. Harriet said her husband suspects her of still having a romantic interested in Franks. She swears they've remained friendly and continue a business relationship, but she's never been with Franks since she and Rose became engaged."

Bree nodded. "That makes sense. I had a strange feeling there was more to those fellas' hostility than business dealings."

"Your gut wasn't wrong. It's a good thing you trusted it and told me. I might never have found out."

"What's going to happen to Rose?" The guy was a crook and possibly a killer.

"We're continuing the investigation, but a judge has issued a warrant for his arrest. We'll be picking him up tomorrow. I'm sure he'll lose his position, and he'll serve time for embezzlement. We're looking into the possibility of Harriet's involvement and whether either or both could be connected to the Franks murder."

She breathed a heavy sigh. It was her turn to divulge gut-wrenching info. "Thank you, Rex. I appreciate you following those clues and giving me an update."

"Of course, Bree. I told you we will investigate all leads, regardless of where they go. I just never suspected to uncover a crooked politician in the process."

"I've got some important information to share as well."

She waited as his groan came over the phone. "Oh, hell no. Tell me you're not playing Nancy Drew."

Putting a lilt into her voice was difficult, but she gave it a shot. "Nope, I doubt a teen snoop would follow clues all the way to New York City."

His voice growled, "You didn't?"

"Actually, I was on a roll and couldn't allow the trail to go cold. So, yes, I went to the Big Apple to meet the female James dined with the evening before the night of his death." She grabbed a quick breath before he could interrupt. Momentum was going. Not the time to waste it. "At the restaurant Mya and I saw them dining at, I learned the gal was from somewhere around the New York area. That led me to the Newport hotel she stayed in. There I obtained her name and address. I flew to New York City to meet with her. We had a very informative discussion."

"How the hell? My…my people questioned restaurant personnel." She visioned him scowling at the other end of the line.

"Not the sommelier." She allowed satisfaction to tinge her words.

"That woman could be the killer. You could've been facing a murderer. What were you thinking?" Rex was reacting exactly as she'd assumed he would.

"I don't believe she is, but I'm sure you're going to want to rule her out yourself."

"Damn straight." Was that admiration, wonder, or bafflement coloring his voice?

"I also have a lead on where James could've hidden his computer and cash. It's too late tonight to go searching for it. Why don't you come over tomorrow morning? I'll make coffee. Bring pastries. Then you and I can go see if I'm right."

A little puff sounded. "Yeah, let's do it."

"Rex, before you come, you might want to do a little online research. Pull up 'New York Franklin C. James' and 'Lola Alessandra.'" She went on to give Rex Lola's address and phone number. "Lola knows you're going to call. It can wait, however, until we look for the money. I'd bet my life on her not being the killer."

"Lola? You sound like old chums and like you already did rule her out." She smiled at his comment, felling no need to answer. He paused a long moment. "Well, guess you better get some sleep. You had quite a day."

He had clearly given up scolding her. It didn't work anyway.

"Good night, Rex. See you in the morning." Giddiness of anticipation fluttered from her chest downward.

Fresh Starts, Dirty Money

CHAPTER NINETEEN

Her bedroom door creaked open stirring Bree from deep sleep. Mya must need her. Her cloudy brain begged to drift back off. That thought went out of her head as a thick, calloused hand slapped across her mouth.

Adrenaline surged through her veins. Eyes shot wide open with a smothered gasp. Nostrils flared. Her mind attempted to flip to panic mode, but she focused enough to recall what she'd learned at defense classes she'd taken about self-preservation.

Breath. Remain Calm. Fight or flight. It's best to run if you can. Fight if you must.

"Mya?" She mouthed the question against the rough paw.

A skinny, tall male with a rounded back and what looked like a permanent slump, shoved Mya from her own bedroom into the hallway. She glanced wide-eyed into Bree's room before the punk pushed her toward the stairwell.

"She's fine. So are you. You'll both stay that way if you cooperate." Her intruder's gruff, deep, New Yorker twang told her all she needed to know. *Frank James' killers*. He didn't sound deranged. Maybe she could reason with him.

Head spinning with thoughts, she was yanked from beneath silky covers to a sitting position. "We're going downstairs to have a little chat. Do not fight. Do not scream. Your lives depend on it." A pistol barrel's nose jammed into her ribs.

She winced. That was going to bruise.

Instead of protesting, she slid her feet into fuzzy slippers beside her bed and stood. He nudged her forward, and she trudged toward the stairs. The overhead lighting had been flipped on in the living room.

What did they want with her and Mya?

Together and with the barrel against her back, she led him to the living room. Mya sat trembling in a chair on one side of the mantle.

A skinny guy in need of a shave and haircut leaned his back against the banister, wearing a dark tee shirt, baggy jeans, and dirty sneakers. Light glinted against a long, slim blade casually held in one of his gnarly fingers.

Meeting Bree's eyes corners of her mouth went slightly up, willing hope to her precious aunt. Breen needed to be strong for her.

Mia's lips pursed. She batted moisture from her eyes. "Do as they say, Bree. We're going to be fine."

Mia might be a petite, little thing, but she had more courage than Bree had anticipated.

With a brief nod she walked past her aunt to a chair her intruder pointed at. With his shove to her back, she stumbled. As she caught herself against a table beside the sofa and stood upright the lamp seated there toppled and pitched to the floor crashing against ceramic tile in front of the fireplace.

Instinct lodged Bree forward to try and catch it. Burly Man jerked her by the arm and, with little effort, plopped her behind into the chair. The light fixture shattered. Shards of glass scattered across the carpeting. "Sit the fuck down."

Mya's chin rose. "If it's money you want, I don't carry much cash. What I have is in my handbag over there." She pointed to the hallway table. "Take my credit cards."

If only that was what they were after. Bree gave it a whirl. "My purse is upstairs. There are a few hundred dollars in my wallet, but I only have one credit card. It's probably maxed out." It had been a costly day.

Chunky Guy snickered. "Nice, but we're not here for your piddly, little change. We want the money Frank James stole from our pa. That son-of-a-bitch took everything our old man made in his long career as a longshoreman. When that thieving snake disappeared with Pa's dough, the old guy couldn't take it. He hung himself. James owes us big money— not pocket change."

Mya frowned, a spunky look in her eyes. "Why are you bothering us? We only learned today he was a thief." Mya was putting on a beautiful front, but it wasn't working on these guys.

"We know better. You broads know where James hid the stash, and you're going to get it for us—that is, if you want to see daylight." He turned to his partner. "Zach, get the bug in the kitchen."

"Ah, Burt, you shouldn't a ought a used my name." Skinny Dude, Zach, strolled into the kitchen, pulled something small from beneath the bar, and pocketed it. Chunky, Burt, reached beneath the coffee table and pocketed the listening device hidden there.

"Shut up and do it, Zach. The Feds will figure out soon enough who we are. By then cabana girls will be serving us umbrella drinks on a private beach. The fuzz won't find these pretty ladies until tomorrow."

Mya's nostrils flared, and she snapped, "You bugged my house? When? How?"

Burt shrugged, shoulders rocking back, and chin held high. "Easy. You broads are gone all day. Your door locks are a joke, and we've got a few skills up our sleeves. Little Bro here procured us a couple of these babies from his previous employment at a techy shop. We slipped in, planted our toys, and slipped out. You were none the wiser."

They may have tools, but they are not wise. Maybe wise asses, but they were low on creativity and brains. It could be helpful if Bree could reason with them. If they were careless and rash, the perilous situation Bree and Mya could become even more extreme.

Mya gushed. "You killed Jimmy?" Frank James would probably always be Jimmy to her.

Burt wasn't done bragging. "We didn't kill him— just a little torture incentive. Dumb shit died before he could give up the money. Couldn't take the pain. Croaked right there on his desktop. Searching didn't turn up his dough. We figured you dames might know where he hid it, or your copper boyfriend might say something helpful."

They had heard everything she'd told Mya and Rex. No need for Bree to deny she had an idea how to locate the missing cash.

Burt glared at Bree. "My brother is going to take your aunt to a safe location. You're going to find that dough for us. If I don't call Zach to say I have the moola by two a.m., he's going to use that switchblade of his to slice her lily-white throat."

Mya gasped. Zach flashed his knife in a swirl through the air with a snicker. Then, with a wink, he snatched Mya's arm and tugged her to her feet. "We're going on a date, beautiful."

Mya shrunk in size before Bree's eyes, then bravely stood tall as her build allowed. "Listen. You harm one hair on my head, you'll be sorry."

Zach's eyes showed he saw it for the empty threat it was. He pushed Mya toward the garage door, stopping by the entryway to snatch the keyring beside Mya's purse.

Burt pulled Bree to her feet. "Let's go get the money, honey."

She forced her lungs to breath in and out at a normal rate—not easy with an automatic pistol pointed at her back. "We can give it a go, but I only have an idea where it might be. I don't know anything for sure."

"It's okay, doll. I've got confidence in you. Whatever you were going to show that cop boy-toy, you'll show me first."

"Are you going to kill us?" If they intended to do it anyway, why bother? Make it harder on them.

"Hope not. If you cooperate, your aunt will be left safely tied up where she'll be found tomorrow. I assume you and I are going to James' house. You'll be left tied up there for the cops to find. If you force me to go to Plan B by not cooperating, you'll have a bullet to your head." He rustled her wild curls. "It would be a shame to mess these pretty locks up with dried blood."

In the garage, Zach pushed Mya into the driver's seat. He went around and climbed in beside her. The door still open, his words came out loud and clear as he pushed his knife toward Mya. "Don't go getting any ideas about crashing the car or anything else as stupid. This little baby will slide inside your skinny ribs like a carving knife through a tender pork loin. Easy-peasy. Got it?"

Mya nodded looking like she was holding tears back.

"Alright then. Drive the speed limit. Follow directions. Be a good girl. You'll live to see your niece again." Again, Mya silently nodded then glanced at Bree with shaded eyes.

Burt shut the car and opened the garage door. Mya backed out slowly then drove off down the street. Burt nudged Bree forward, and they exited the way the car had. He hit the button inside the doorway, and the automatic closer engaged, bringing it down slowly. Once it closed, he pointed his pistol toward the James house.

She would get further with her captor with a bit of cooperation than argument. Might as well start the ball rolling. "So, Burt, how are we getting into the house? The police have it locked up and their crime scene tape around it."

The big dude shrugged. "Ah, me and Zach been in the joint a half a dozen times since that thieving rattlesnake croaked. We just left the doors unlocked. I don't think the fuzz have been back. They got what they wanted outta there the day they found old Frankie swinging in the breeze." She gave a slight choking sound.

He grunted. "Sorry, babe, forgot you was the one who discovered him. Them's the brakes. Let's get to it, Doll." Wrapping one burly arm around her shoulders, he pushed his weapon into her ribs'; and they began to walk. "If anyone stops us or says anything, we're just a couple out for a lovers' stroll."

A shiver sped down her spine. *Yewee.*

It had to be nearing midnight. A glance at the alarm clock on her bedside table when she'd awoken had shown eleven-forty-five p.m. "Yeah, sure. I always go strutting around the neighborhood in my pajamas after a satisfying roll in the hay." A shudder rocked her shoulders.

"Funny gal. I like a female with a sense of humor." They made it to James' front door without meeting anyone. Probably, the neighbors were soundly sleeping, like she should be instead of treasure hunting with a vengeful maniac.

Fresh Starts, Dirty Money

CHAPTER TWENTY

Rex researched the names Bree had given him on his laptop. It had taken an enlightening couple of hours sitting at his dining room table. From what he read, Lola Alessandra, James' housemate and lover, had been cleared by the FBI of wrongdoing. Far as they could tell, she'd been unaware of his embezzlement until after he disappeared, only informed when Suits moved in.

Bree had sounded confident Alessandra wasn't involved in the murder. Possibly, the killer found James by watching her. If so, they could now be following Bree, too. If that was the case, she and Mya could be in danger. He was ready to call the station to put a protective detail on them when his phone buzzed.

His sister's kid, Lee Walters' picture showed on the screen. He clicked the call open. "Hey. What's up, Lee? Aren't you working?"

It was unusual to hear from the young man, especially at this hour. The kid worked as a desk clerk at a downtown hotel in the evenings. They were flexible about his schedule, to accommodate college classes he took most mornings. Second shift allowed Lee to study during down time.

"Yeah, I'm at the hotel now. That's why I'm calling. There's something suspicious you might want to check on."

Rex continued perusing the computer screen, giving his nephew only half of his attention. "All right. What is it?" Probably someone sneaking a prostitute into the hotel.

"It was slow this evening, so I took trash from the offices out around midnight. As I tossed it into the dumpster out back a dark sedan showed up. Real nice car—expensive. A man got out of the passenger seat. I recognized him as a guest, but he's always been with this big, strong-looking man when I've seen him before. Anyway, the guy went around and kind of roughhoused a woman out of the driver's seat. She looked like that friend of yours who owns the lady's shop at the mall. I think her name is Ms. Landry or Laundry."

A bad feeling sank into Rex's gut. His nephew's call received his full focus. "It's Landry. Why is that suspicious. Maybe they're on a date."

He pictured the kid smirking on the other end. "Uncle Rex, I know a booty call when I see one. We have 'em all the time at the hotel. A gal usually gets all gussied up if she's going to make it with a dude.

This wasn't that. Ms. Landry wasn't wearing makeup. Her hair was a mess, and she was wearing a nightgown and robe. That's no date."

That sinking feeling had turned to grinding, spiky wheels in Rex's stomach. He swallowed a golf ball-sized lump lodged in his throat. No sense alarming the kid. "Sounds right. Anything else?"

"The guy left earlier with the big dude. They both have key cards. When this one returned with the woman, he used his room key to enter the hotel's back door. It's required after ten p.m. They went immediately to the elevator bank and took one to their floor. I followed them inside and checked surveillance cameras for their level. They went to the room he shares with his buddy. and he shoved her inside kind of harshly. I'm keeping the camera on that floor so I can keep an eye out for any change, but they haven't left."

Rex took a slow, deep inhale. This wasn't good. Mya Landry was extremely proper and discreet. She preferred men more sophisticated than this person sounded. "Okay, here's what you do. Keep an eye on their door. If either of them leaves, note the time and where they go. Under no circumstances are you to say anything to him that might indicate you're suspicious. I'm sending someone right over. Sit tight. When my people show, inform them of any changes. Give them access to the room and anything else they need. Then stay out of their way. They'll handle this."

His sister would skin Rex alive if something happened to her kid on his watch. Besides, he loved the little guy.

"Thanks, Uncle Rex. I knew you'd know what to do, or you'd tell me if I was just being paranoid."

Rex blew out a breath. "You're not being paranoid. You did good, Lee. Really good. You're keeping your eyes peeled for oddities. That's a good thing. Thanks, and stay safe."

"I will, Uncle Rex, and thank you."

"You bet." Rex clicked off and dialed the SWAT team. As he explained what to do, he pulled his flak jacket on and attached his utility belt. After he hung up, he checked his weapons and then called his office.

Officer Izzy Comings answered. "Hey, Chief, why are you up at this hour?"

"We've got an emergency. Who else is on duty and available?"

Her soft voice belied her fierce protective nature when it came to Newport citizens. "Rusty Martin and Van Carter are here."

"Good. Tell Carter to take over the phones. I want you and Martin to meet me at the address I'm texting you. Park around the corner and walk over to the front. I'll meet you there. No lights, no siren. We want to surprise the perps." While he talked, he strode to his garage. Leaving the cruiser in place, he opted for his pickup truck—less conspicuous.

"Got 'cha, Chief." We'll be there in ten minutes."

Seven minutes later he parked halfway down the block from Mya's house. As he walked up the driveway, he was met by Officers Izzy Comings and Rusty Martin. "Thanks for coming. I have a suspicion of a house invasion at this address. Evidence leads me to believe one female resident has been taken to another location. SWAT is on that lead now. The other female resident is either being held captive in this house or at the crime scene across the street." He glanced at the darkened house behind him, still swathed with drooping crime scene tape. The James house upstairs master faced the back of the building, so it was not visible. Blinds and drapes were drawn on the picture window in front—the living room.

Rex gave a head nod toward Mya's home. "We'll try here first. Rusty, you take the back door. We'll take the front."

They acknowledged Rex's orders with a head bob. Mya's and Bree's kitchen and living room lights were on, but Bree and her captor could be anywhere.

He pulled his weapon from its holster and eased the screen door soundlessly open. Izzy stood ready and gun drawn at his back. The doorknob turned easily, unlocked.

Not good.

He held it for a deep breath then shoved it open, pointing his pistol in the room and yelling, "NPD," to the empty room.

Izzy stepped in behind him, and they split apart checking different areas of the space they'd invaded. She searched the living room. He cleared the stairwell then checked the coat closet and moved toward the dining area as Rusty opened and exploded into the kitchen with another yell of, "NPD."

Rex called, "Clear." Rusty joined him in the dining area.

Izzy added, "Clear," and joined them in the dining room while Rusty cleared the pantry and kitchen.

Izzy screwed lips to the side. "Chief, there's a broken lamp in the living room. No blood."

He nodded and breathed a sigh of relief, but it was short lived as he glanced toward the foyer table. "Mya's purse is on the entryway table. She'd never leave it. Proves she didn't go to that hotel willingly."

That was SWAT's case. His case was to find Bree and arrest whomever had her. This hadn't been a delusion on his part. It was real. Bree and Mya were in danger. He shoved concern down into another compartment of his mind to be delt with later. He had a job to do and couldn't afford to let worry get the better of him.

"Upstairs, Izzy, follow me. Rusty, keep watch down here." Rusty was a great cop but less experienced than Izzy. Rex would partner with her anytime, knowing she had his back.

He took steps carefully. She followed his lead, leaning their backs against the side wall rising one stair at a time. Weapons pointed toward the second floor. Having never been upstairs in Mya's house, he wasn't sure of the layout.

The bathroom door stood ajar. Izzy stepped in and flipped the shower curtain aside then gave him a shake of her head.

The first doorway was open. Rex's weapon pointed toward anyone who might be occupying the space as he stepped inside. Izzy came in and flicked the light on. Covers were pushed aside on the unmade bed. Indentation in the pillow showed it had been slept in. Rex moved into the master bath, searched, and declared it, "Clear." Izzy did the same for the walk-in closet.

Returning to the hallway, they moved to the last bedroom. Izzy led, opening the half-open door with her backside, and scanning the empty room. Rex flipped the light on. Bree's purse sat on the dresser. Her phone laid on the bedside table.

Pain shot into his gut. It couldn't have been worse had he been stabbed.

Bree had been taken. No denying it now.
He had to get her back—safely and alive.

CHAPTER TWENTY-ONE

The knob turned easily. Burt nudged her inside then shut the door behind them. To the left of the entryway, blinds and drapes were drawn in the living room. That should block most of the light, assuming Burt turned them on. Neighbors would need to be extremely nosey to realize something was amiss.

"So, Little Lady, where do we begin?" An eager glare crossed his puffy cheeks.

"Upstairs. What we're looking for is likely to be in his bedroom. He would want to keep it close." She blinked away fear threatening to control her, seriously doubting it was upstairs; but she needed to stall as long as possible.

He shoved her toward the stairs and boldly flipped on the lights. They first checked the guest bedroom to rule it out. No furniture, only a few weights and a treadmill occupied the room. Nothing in the closet. The house's drywalled rooms didn't lend themselves to providing hiding spaces. The guest bath was similar. Easy to tell it was rarely used. Toilet paper, hand soap and there was a clean towel hanging on the rack.

The master bedroom was also sparsely furnished with a four-poster, modern bed of black iron. Side shelves supplied space for an alarm clock. Lamps attached to the wall above each shelf. No dresser or chest of drawers. A flat-screened television attached to a metal arm along the wall opposite the bed. No place to hide anything.

She looked behind the single painting in the room and found nothing. "Help me flip the mattress over, so we can check for a compartment."

Might as well make a pretense of searching wherever someone might've hidden their stash. Burt didn't act as though he doubted it would be in such a location, only eager to locate it.

She stood on one side eyeing the hulky man across from her. Without argument, he helped her turn over the California King-sized mattress. She let him do the bulk of the muscle work. They inspected all four sides and the bottom but found nothing. Box springs were the same. Exhausting opportunities there, they plopped the mattress back into place.

She sat on one edge staring with a critical eye at the man who held her captive. "If you didn't kill Frank James, how did he die?" This guy had no clue she knew the gory details of Frank's torture. She needed to get him used to talking to her, build a relationship.

His cheek tweaked a near wink. "That dumb shit refused to turn over the dough, so we hurt him a little to convince him we were serious. Little wimp couldn't take it. He croaked before he could fess up where he stashed it."

"You hurt him a little? How so?" She acted interested in him and his story. Most people liked to talk about themselves. Intending to give him every chance to do that, she took advantage of the big lug's having no idea she was aware he and his brother had brutalized James into having cardiac arrest.

Burt's shoulders rolled back, and his chest heaved high. "Me and Zach clipped his nails one at a time."

"By nails, I assume you mean fingertips." She allowed her brows to rise and cocked a brow with a cool stare.

He shrugged, like it was no big deal. "Yeah, we cut off a little above the nail line. We're not professional manicurists, you know." He chuckled at his macabre humor.

She let her eyes go wide to appear in awe. Her mouth went into an O. "So, he didn't appreciate the spa treatment and died. Wow, you must've been disappointed."

His head rocked side-to-side. "You got no idea, Lady."

"Wow, it must've been hard cutting through bone like that."

"Nah, if you slice through the knuckle," he touched his to show her where, "a good blade slices clean through."

She tilted her head. "So, you must've come prepared with the right tool."

His brows rose. "Actually, I was but I found this awesome gadget in Old Frankie's cigar box." He whipped a shiny object from his pants pocket. "This little baby made it clear sailing—sliced right through the knuckle like nobody's business." He moved the cigar cutter around, letting overhead lighting glint on its shiny surface, as he admired his bounty.

"That's James' cigar cutter?"

Burt shrugged and stowed the tool in his trousers. "Guess so."

"My aunt told me Mr. James had bought an expensive one at an exclusive New York auction house for a large sum of money. It belonged to Frank Sinatra. Documentation stated that John F. Kennedy had it made as a gift especially for the singer."

Burt's eyes popped. "No shit? I have Old Blue Eyes' cigar cutter?" He nodded several times toward the ceiling as though giving himself a pat on the back.

She'd gotten out of him where the cigar cutter had disappeared to and confirmed it was the murder weapon, and he'd admitted to torturing James to death. She was on a roll. Her brow furrowed, as though she trying to understand. "If James was already dead, why go to the trouble to hang him in that empty lot?"

He shot her a toothy grin. "That was brilliant. Don't you think? It was an ironic salute to our pa. Our old man worked a derrick on the docks his whole life. I'll just bet Pa's rolling around in his coffin laughing at that stroke of genius."

She nodded as though understanding his witty plan. "Why use that silk scarf?"

A broad smile proved she was getting into his head. "Oh, that was another clever notion I came up with. That pretty, little trophy was tied to the bedpost. I figured it would send 'em searching for Frankie Boy's lover. Keep the cops busy trying to figure out who did it. Maybe throw them off their game. Give us more time to find the dough. Smart, huh?"

She let her brows rise, as she nodded with wide eyes. "Oh, yeah. It worked alright. They've been barking up every wrong tree around. No clue about you and Zach."

He didn't mention Lola Alessandra. By lover, did he mean her or Mya?

"You must be super intelligent to come up with all these clever strategies. I guess you're the brains of this operation—so to speak." She stood, wanting to move around before he got antsy.

"You could say that." He boasted, chest out. "Little Bro is bright when it comes to electronics and such. He's good at video games, technology, and the internet. When it comes to real life situations and concocting plans, it's all me. Zach's an introvert. Worked in a shop his whole adult life. Never had a steady broad. I'm probably his only friend." His shoulders rocked back. "Now me? I'm more worldly. Manning the docks like our pa. Hanging with real men. Not namby-pamby twerps in a fantasy land."

Her head lolled back. "Oh yeah, I could tell. You've been around. It shows." *Around one too many pizzas, seeing much of the world through beer goggles.*

He pointed. "Let's check the bathroom."

The oversized, master bath had a water closet, shower stall, and a claw-footed tub. A lone soap dispenser sat on the double vanity. She squatted and peeked beneath the sink. A partial bag of toilet paper rolls, a pump bottle of cleanser, a can of spray disinfectant, and a squeeze bottle of toilet bowl cleaner.

If she squirted him in the eyes with it, would the bottle cooperate. Would she be able to get away? Maybe, but that would leave Mya hanging.

No dice.

Rooting around she ruled out the idea of a hidden compartment there. They inspected the mirror hanging above the vanity in lieu of a medicine cabinet.

He grunted. "It's securely attached to the wall. No way to remove it except with power tools." Nothing there.

Linen closet metal shelving held several square baskets. One contained personal hygiene items—toothpaste, toothbrush, deodorant, aftershave, cologne, brush, comb, nail clippers, a can of hair spray, and a tub of male skin moisturizer. A second hosted a row of neatly rolled, white and a stack of pale grey wash cloths. Plush towels sat on the shelving beside it.

"Nothing hidden there." Stooping, she inspected behind and under the tub. "Nothing there."

She stood, stretched, and put hands on hips then closed the door. "Why are you doing this to us? Mya and I didn't even know you guys existed. We've done nothing to you."

His mouth squirreled left. What looked like regret showed in his murky eyes. His thick voice sounded much like his eyes. Burt appeared to be second-guessing his decisions. "We got nothing against you broads. We just want what is rightfully ours."

She needed to appeal to his emotions. "What about your mom? Aren't you leaving her high and dry, running off with your dad's investment? What will happen to her? No money. No husband. No sons? Won't she be miserable never seeing you again?"

Boys adored their mothers. Right?

His lips squeezed together. "Ma passed away when we were little. Pa raised us. He was all we had. Now he's gone, and so is his money." These guys clearly, depended on their father for guidance and never quite grew into their own independence. Two middle-aged, co-dependent dopes raised by an enabling parent. Trying to make up for their not having a mother, he'd done them no service.

James Franks or Frankie James had done awful things to many people, these two included. Fallout from his disastrous crimes continued to show its miserable head. Burt and Zach's dad must've been at his lowest point to have committed suicide.

Against her wishes, a pang of sympathy hit her. "I'm sorry for your loss, Burt. I lost my own mother recently, and before that, my dad." People liked being called by name. She was willing to use psychology to work this man, regardless how he'd suffered.

"Please, don't take it out on my aunt or me. James fooled Mya, too. They were seeing each other. Mya thought he was a good, honest man. She loved him and is grieving his loss. He's done almost the same thing to her that he did to you. Don't make her suffer more than she already is."

What looked like anger flashed in his dark eyes. "She ain't lost nothing. That SOB would've taken off with the dough and left her behind. She's better off without him."

"A point we agree on. You're right. She is better off without him, but her heart is broken. Don't hurt her. I'll do my best to find the money, but it's not all yours. James stole from over three-hundred people. The bulk of that belongs to them. I'm sure the FBI will distribute the recovered funds to all rightful owners once they find it. You should inherit your father's part. Why don't you let them handle this?"

There was some good in him. She could see it, or what she assumed his thoughtful expression meant. Or was he too far gone for reasoning?

His cheeks puffed out. "We ain't waiting. Can't trust the Feds. I don't feel sorry for them other schmucks. They ain't got the guts to go after what is theirs. So be it."

One of her brows shot high. "You must realize, Burt, you're wrong about one thing. Taking that money makes you and Zach as bad as Frank James. I don't think you and your brother are the criminal type."

Her head pulled back anticipating how he might react. Best get out of arm's reach.

What did she know? She hoped her words weren't complete fabrications.

He twitched. "It's too late for us. James is dead. We're taking that dough and skipping town. They'll never find us."

She studied him for a few seconds. "Don't you think that's what Frank James believed, too? That the authorities would never find him. They always do…eventually. Besides, you haven't actually murdered anyone . . . yet. You could get off easily, especially if Mya and I testified on your behalf."

Hopefully, putting that bug into his brain might eventually take hold. She had no idea if what she proposed was legitimate, but it was worth a try.

He glared. "They didn't. Me and Zach did. It's ours."

She was curious. "How did you find Frank James, anyway?"

He looked self-satisfied. "We been tailing that pretty piece of tail he left behind in New York. Figured she'd eventually lead us to him, and she did. We kept a surveillance detail on her for years. Finally panned out. Spent nearly every extra penny we made to pay the private dick."

She pushed her brows high. "Wow, that's dedication." Too bad they hadn't aimed that intense focus on building their own careers and fortune.

Burt shrugged. "It was the best we could do— better odds than buying a lottery ticket. It was tough though, paying that expense for so long. I figure we're owed."

These dudes clearly didn't have a life. "Don't you guys have jobs you need to get back to?"

He gave her a one-sided grin. "Not anymore. We're here to cash in on our investment. Now, let's get at it." Did he hear the irony in his description?

Doubtful.

CHAPTER TWENTY-TWO

Bree stumbled toward the hallway as Burt pushed. She'd been stalling for time to find a way out of the perilous predicament she was in, feeling more and more like a caged monkey in an experimental lab.

She wasn't about to leave Mya in danger. Her only hope was to learn where Zach was holding Mya and escape Burt's watchful eyes in time to rescue her aunt.

Last resort, she'd locate the money for Burt and hope he and his brother were sincere about not wanting to harm them. She didn't believe he was a hardcore murderer, but he had employed brutal torture trying to eek the cash's location out of Frank James. Once you'd killed, did it become easier? Was she hoping in vain to live through this night?

As she'd searched, she'd looked for anything she could use as a weapon, planning to conceal the object, whatever it might be, until an optimal time to use it. She wasn't leaving Burt without knowing where Mya was, and she'd not gotten that out of her captor yet. She was running out of time.

Burt followed close behind as she thoughtfully took the open-stepped stairway. Its modern construction and metal railing provided no safe hiding place for the treasure Burt wanted her to find.

Turning right, she left the entryway. Glass tables flanked a sofa in the sparsely decorated living room. No television. She pulled out the lone painting that hung on the wall and looked behind it. Nothing.

She glanced at her kidnapper. "Help me check the sofa."

Without argument, the big lug went to the opposite end and flipped the couch upside down. There was nothing below or on any of its sides. They turned it up right again and inspected the base. Nothing. Unzipping each cushion, they found naught.

She tossed one into place. "It's not in here. All these rooms are carpeted. He couldn't have hidden anything under the floor. Let's try the kitchen. I have an idea." She didn't, but he didn't know that.

The pantry held a mop, broom, dustpan, and bucket propped against its back corner. Few groceries sat on a metal shelf—typical bachelor. Again, drywall provided no hiding opportunity. Returning to the kitchen, she ceremoniously searched each cabinet, pulling out every drawer and moving items around.

Finishing with the last lower cabinet, she stood and stretched. "Mr. James wasn't much of a cook, from what I see."

Burt shrugged with a snarl. "Dude is from New York. Probably got takeout."

He helped search drawers and cabinets but watched her like a mother hen with a baby chick, when it came to checking drawers. Probably thought she'd find a knife and pull it on him. She could visibly see him counting their number every time she encountered a blade.

She got on her knees and inspected the range, which appeared to have never been used. "Nothing here."

"Son-of-a-bitch." Burt's face turned pink, and he blew out a huff. The big boy was getting tired of this tedious task. She'd best get what she needed soon, or she and Mya would be the Jersey Boys' next victims.

She stood and walked to the side-by-side refrigerator. Opening the freezer first, she gazed around. An ice pick mounted to a spot beside the container that caught cubes from the ice maker caught her eye. She slipped a hand over it, covering it so Burt had no chance to see it. Making a production of rustling icy cubes, as though hunting for something hidden there, she palmed the tool.

Without facing her companion, she shut the door and opened the refrigerator side. "Nothing in there but a couple of steaks."

He chuckled, as though they were on a date, and he was trying to be entertaining. "It's a shame to waste good beef, but who has time to cook?"

"Hey, there's beer in here. Want one?" She glanced over her shoulder.

"Sure." He reached a beefy mitt her way. She put an icy, brown bottle in it. "James had expensive taste in brew."

He twisted the cap to no avail. "Damn stuff needs an opener."

She nodded toward the pantry without turning toward him. "I saw one attached to a wall over the trash can in the pantry."

Burt strutted into the pantry to open his beer. Heart racing, she slid the icepick into the elastic waistband of her underwear and concealed her weapon with her pajama top. Now for an optimal time to use it.

Burt returned and took a long swig. "Sister, we've exhausted this room. Only place left to search is the office.

They'd eventually had to go there, but she'd been putting it off until last. James' stash had to be in that room since it wasn't in James' bedroom, the two locations she figured it could be. Searching the rest of the house was her way of stalling, buying time to gather information, and looking for something to defend herself.

"Look, Hon, time's a running out. Your pretty, little auntie is going to wind up with a bloody neckline if you don't find that money soon. I don't want to kill you. You seem like a nice gal and all. But I'll put a hot one in your brain if I need to, in order to get out of town safely. Just find me that dough, and I'll leave you alone."

"Where's my aunt? I need to know where to find her." She glared.

One of his shoulders rose and fell. "No worries. Someone will discover her tomorrow. It's a sure thing."

"Why? Where is she? It won't hurt to tell me. I'll be tied up here until someone realizes I'm missing and comes looking." She strolled out of the kitchen, her back to him.

"Housekeeping will find the old gal when they clean up. They'll call the fuzz. Your aunt knows where I took you. So, no need to worry your pretty head. You'll both be rescued safe and sound, assuming you get me that dough." Confidence coated his voice.

She wished she was as sure she and Mya would survive this gig.

Housekeeping?

Mya was at a hotel. Were they seriously dumb enough to put her in their hotel room? Must not be afraid the police would learn their identities. *Which one?*

What were the chances Burt had checked into the same hotel Lola Alessandra had stayed out? *Possibly.* They followed her here and would've wanted to stay close by to watch her every move.

Her deadline was getting tight. It was one-thirty, according to the clock on the kitchen range. Bree had about a half hour.

No one had come to rescue Bree. She had no hope they would. Mya was the only person who knew she was in danger. If Bree couldn't get away soon, they were screwed.

Burt waved a hand toward the small restroom to the right near the kitchen. "I've got to drain the old lizard. That beer went right through me. You sit and stay put." He strolled to the guest washroom and turned his back, leaving the door open behind him. "I've never figured out how eight measly ounces of brew can equal a couple gallons of piss." He chuckled, and the sound of his zipper eased through the open door.

"Beer does that to me, too." She kept her voice conversational.

Tinkle of his slow flow melded with her thoughts. She plopped onto a cushioned seat, elbows on knees and head in hands. It was time to act. She must focus, alert for any opportunity to escape. Hope was draining faster from her than the slow trickle of piss passing a likely swollen prostrate in the water closet. She hadn't been as desperate since the day she'd witnessed Owen bonking his paralegal on his desktop, the woman's skinny legs wrapped around her husband's waist.

That horrible day after that fun-filled episode of 'Bree, Crashed and Burned', alternately titled 'The Bree Collins Soap Opera,' Bree had made necessary stops on the way home. Finally, once there, she stood naked in the shower, scalding water splashing over her flesh and washing away her life as it slowly trickled down the drainpipe like Burt's urine trickled into the guest John. Hope of living through this night and saving her aunt drizzled away in much the same manner, as he kept a watchful eye over his shoulder for his captive.

She'd had no opportunity to escape yet. She shuddered the gruesome image in her mind of her and Mya dead at the hands of the derelict brothers.

A rush of adrenaline surged into her vanes. She'd found a weapon and figured out where Mya was being held. That was two-out-of-three. There was still a chance. Maybe if she turned the cash over to Burt, he'd be preoccupied with his treasure and forget about her long enough for her to escape. Surely, if she could get outside the house, she could find a place to hide until she could get help. Maybe wake a neighbor.

Her head rose. She stared at entrances to the two rooms in the back of the house. A set of French doors in the office led to the back yard. *Escape route?* To the right was the kitchen. To the left was the office, the last place to search, and probably where the treasure was well-concealed.

Two things got her attention. Movement flashed outside the kitchen door. *Animal?* Had a nosey, insomniac neighbor realized lights were on in the vacant murder house? Hopefully, they would enlist help, instead of checking the place out alone. She didn't want a good Samaritan walking into danger unaware.

Sure, she had figured out where Frank James had hidden his ill-gotten currency, she pushed forward before fear took hold of her. "Have you and Zach been able to check out any of the local sites while you've been in town?" Maybe meaningless, chatty conversation would keep his less-than keen mind busy.

"Nah. At first, we were trailing that Italian chick. Then there was our little '*Come to Jesus*' meeting with Frankie James. Afterward, we've spent most of our time nosing through this joint or following you and your aunt." He paused for a second. Dribble stopped, replaced by rake of his zipper being pulled into place. "All we've seen was a bunch of tall buildings and a river—about the same as home. There was fireworks one night, though." Sound of water running signaled washing his hands. He'd soon return to her and the search.

They must've stayed at a riverfront hotel. A breath of relief came. It had to be the one Lola had occupied. "The Reds shoot them off when they hit a home run or win a game."

Burt slothed into the living room with a slap of his hands and a grin. "Let's get at it. Time's a wasting." Truer words were never spoken.

Still, she needed to stall before resorting to an effort to escape. If someone had called for help it could be on the way. More than likely, what she'd seen was a stray dog running by the window.

She was on her own. No way could Bree overpower the muscular man who stood a head taller than her. She needed to be choiceful about how to go about this.

It was time to face the scene where James had died. Pushing the gory aspect of it out of her mind was the only way to do what was necessary. With a deep inhale, she followed Burt as he switched overhead lights on.

It wasn't a large room. Just enough space for a workable setup. French doors provided entry between living room and office, and a set exited to the back patio. Side walls housed built-in, wooden cabinets and shelving both behind the desk and on the opposite wall.

A modern desktop without drawers sat closer to the left side. A navy, leather, executive chair backed up to the left side wall of cabinets. Two navy, leather, guest chairs faced the desk on the other side. Tall plants flanked exit doors to the back yard. *Locked?*

A forty-inch, flat-screen television was mounted inside a large cubicle in the shelving unit opposite the desk. Art pieces and an impressive book display decorated the rest of the sections. The unit to the left held similar items. One segment contained James' infamous humidor.

Dark, crusty, dried, blood caked on the far side of the otherwise pristine desktop. Bree suppressed a cringe. *Ignore it. Focus on what's important. You can't do anything for James, and Mya needs you.*

She strolled casually to the chair and sat. The willies ran down her spine. She cinched the shiver of her shoulders as they reacted on impulse, and then began the 'act' of searching for a lever or button that might unlock a hidden alcove.

"So, Burt, you and Zach haven't really killed anyone yet. Why don't you guys just go home? Let me get that money to the FBI, so they can dispense it to the rightful owners. You and Zach will get your dad's share. James made a considerable profit on this subdivision, so he has at least doubled your dad's investment. That ought to be plenty money for you and your brother to live a nice life on, and you wouldn't spend the rest of your lives on the run. Wouldn't that be better? You can tie me up and leave now. Call Zach and tell him you're moving to Plan C. I'm sure you can sell him on the idea. Your brother obviously looks up to you. It's for his own good. You need to look out for your little bro, Burt. Don't lead him into a life of crime. Just tie me up. By the time I'm found, you'll be safely at home. I'll tell the authorities I don't know who you were. I can even give them a wrong description of you. Come on, Burt. I don't want this to end badly for you." She furrowed her brow trying to look concerned. Not difficult since she was. Why did she care? These guys wouldn't lose sleep over killing her and Mya.

He watched her face as she pleaded. A slow, tender smile crossed his closed lips. A thick finger came out to push an errant curl from her forehead. "You're really sweet, Bree. You know that? I appreciate you worrying about me, and all. It's too late. We've gone too far." The sensitive look left his face with an exhaled gush and stern voice. "Now, get your sweet ass in gear and find that moolah."

She squatted to check the lower shelving. Burt remained in her peripheral vision, and she kept conversation light but ongoing. Her only hope was to distract him and keep him off his guard.

CHAPTER TWENTY-THREE

Rex put hands to his hips and studied the two officers, having finished searching Mya's house to no avail. "Miss Collins and Miss Landry were clearly taken, as we suspected. We know where Miss Landry is being held hostage. SWAT is on that rescue mission. I expected there to be two kidnappers, from the desk clerk's intel. It appears they've split up, one taking each woman. Clearly, the second abductor has Bree Collins. My guess, they're at the James residence."

Rex's phone twitched indicating he'd received a text. He read the message and grinned. "Okay, we're good to go. SWAT's mission was a success, and we're hosting SWAT at the next picnic." He snickered to his people, and they returned nods.

Here's the plan. He outlined how they would approach the scene without being seen. The sky was bright with stars and a half moon, as they followed his instructions to the front of James' residence. Crime scene tape remained sporadically up in place with some blown down or away in others. The police hadn't entered the house since shutting it up after gathering evidence the day after James' murder.

Blinds were drawn on the front window. His team hadn't been left them that way—a sure sign an unauthorized individual had been inside. Vague light shown through the closed blinds. Upstairs windows faced rear. The threesome stood quietly in front of James' closed garage doors, the two officers awaiting Rex's direction.

"Rusty, check the back. Don't show yourself to those inside. Recon and get back here with a report."

Rusty nodded and disappeared around the dark corner. He returned momentarily. "Lights are on upstairs. The kitchen in the back right is lit. It appears the individuals inside have been searching. Place is a mess. Back left room, office, dark. French doors unlocked to that room. Also, kitchen door unlocked. That will make breaching easy from the rear."

Rex nodded without expression. "We left the place completely locked. My guess—they've been inside before and left all the entrances unlocked for their convenience." He stepped to the front door, eased the screen door open, and turned the doorknob in place. It moved easily in his fingers, as he'd expected.

He turned back to his officers. "Unlocked." Rex eased away from the entrance so they could talk. As they moved away, beams showing through drawn blinds brightened with additional illumination coming from the back left. The insiders had moved into the murder room.

He pointed to the corner. "They're in the office— back left. Rusty, go out back. Stay close to the office doors. Don't show yourself. Be prepared. If needed, come through them." He turned to Izzy. "Follow me. Stay behind and watch for my signal. I'm going to try to end this without bloodshed."

Rusty and Izzy nodded. "You got it, Chief."

Rusty disappeared around the side of the building. Izzy tailed close behind Rex. He stealthily stepped to the entrance and again eased the screen door open. Twisting, the knob rotated soundlessly. Veiled voices in the back room came through as he pushed the door forward. No reaction from the occupants signaled it was okay to move in.

Rex entered the lobby with Izzy behind him. He shut the screen door then pushed the heavy, wooden one close, so outside noise wouldn't disturb drama playing out inside. The officers tiptoed to a doorway, and Rex peered around the living room entry.

Bree crouched facing the left outside wall of bookcases. She was conversing nonchalantly with the bulky, carelessly dressed man holding a pistol and towering over her. That was good. Bree was keeping her cool. She'd obviously developed a rapport with her kidnapper.

Relief washed through Rex's chest. He indicated Izzy should come along then slipped into the living room, keeping his back close to the right-side wall, so he couldn't be seen from the office.

Izzy's body heat told him she was near. He crossed the access to the kitchen then stopped at the wall separating it from the office. Turning, he signaled Izzy to stay hidden.

Rex stepped into view of the perpetrator; rifle pointed in the kidnapper's direction. "NPD, hands in the air."

The big man's thick arm shot around Bree's neck, dragging her to her feet and in front of his chest like a shield. His pistol pointed at her temple, head raking sideways. "No dice, Copper. You're not taking me in."

"Put your weapon down. Let the woman go. Let's settle this without you going away for a long stint in the slammer."

"Nah, Copper, you put your weapon down, or your little sweetie ain't going to be so pretty with a hole in her head."

Rex would never give up his only firearm. He had Izzy behind him with her trusty HK416 and Rusty outside with his MP5/10 submachine gun. Plus, Rex was armed with his usual array of concealed weapons on his body. He was willing to give up the rifle, if it kept the big guy talking and distracted, thinking he could buffalo a lone policeman.

Bree mouthed the word, "No," as Rex knelt slowly, hands up and gently laid his Colt M4 carbine rifle down, never taking eyes off her and her captor.

Everything seemed to happen at the same time and in slow motion. Bree's hand slid beneath per pajama top then swung out to the side and back with forceful impact. Light glinted off something shiny gripped tightly in her hand as she plunged it into the man's side.

Simultaneously, the kidnapper's handgun moved from her temple and pointed Rex's direction. With a flash, a cartridge left the chamber and spiraled toward Rex, who was unable to move quick enough to avoid impact.

Bree's knees bend, as she let her weight fall on the man's forearm. He jerked it free with a bellowing scream, as her blade punctured his side. She went to her knees, free from his grip.

This is it.

Something feeling like a semi-truck rammed Rex's chest. Before his eyes, his feet flew up and the ceiling above came into view. Darkness took him.

CHAPTER TWENTY-FOUR

Bree kept Burt talking, but she was nearly finished searching the left side of the room. Soon she'd have to move to the other side. *The money must be over there.*

Mya was doomed if Bree didn't find a way out of this soon. Burt wasn't going to buy her sad or friendly chat act enough to let them go without his sought-after prize. She couldn't win in a battle of strength with the big dude. She would need to give him the money and use cunning to distract him and escape.

Time to give it up.

Hopefully, Burt had one iota of honesty left in him, and that he and Zach were sincere about not wanting to kill her and Mya. If Bree failed to run fast enough to get away when the chance came, it was her only other means of surviving the night. She couldn't count on that.

Before she could rise to a standing position, Rex stormed into the doorway—alone. *What was he thinking? No backup?* A show of force right now might scare her kidnapper into giving up.

Burt's arm yanked her to her feet, bracing her against his chest. His heart pounded the back of her shoulder blades. The men yelled at each other, both firing off orders.

She silently begged Rex not to give up his gun but couldn't get the words out with her airpipe blocked by Burt's hold. Rex held his hands up, his rifle in one, then knelt to lay it on the floor.

Her heart sank to her sour gut. With a gasp she fought for air. At the same time, she slid the ice pick from her panties. Putting all her might into the swing, her arm shot outward and brought the tip into Burt's fleshy leg. The sharp point made contact with the top of his thigh and sunk deep, to the hilt, easier than she'd anticipated. Her knuckles grazed his pants leg as she released the dagger to stay there.

Burt's screech roared in her eardrums. Bree dropped her body's weight against his arm. His grip on her released. She fell to her knees.

Burt's shot blasted so close the air grazed her cheek, and her ears rang. Impact of the slug threw Rex backward with a thud. His head cracked audibly against the floor. She scrambled away from Burt toward Rex's prone, still frame.

A female officer sprang into the doorway. Rifle raised; she fired twice toward Burt.

His scream came at the same time as the outside doors burst open. Bree's head spun around to see a male officer. His rifle posed toward the fallen Burt. He kicked Burt's pistol out of reach and bent to cuff him.

Bree made it to Rex. Her whole body trembled out of control. Her quaking hands scanned his unmoving body.

CHAPTER TWENTY-FIVE

Standing over Bree, the female officer spoke into a hand-held radio device, "Officer down, two injured. Gunshot wounds. Need two ambulances immediately."

Her voice trailed as she gave the address and then disappeared into the kitchen, momentarily returning with a handful of dish towels. She tossed them to the uniformed male who had burst into the room from the patio as the female officer's shots hit their target.

He knelt, crunched over Burt's bleeding frame, putting pressure on the criminal's leaking chest. The officer took the rags and pushed them against Burt's wounds. "Breath is shallow. Two to the chest. Nice shooting, Izzy. How's the Chief?"

The female, Izzy, knelt beside Bree and Rex. "He's out." She peeled Rex's flak jacket away from his torso."

It hadn't occurred to her he'd worn one. *Of course, he had.*

Bree's hands stroked over his front, and she bent to feel his breath on her cheek. She caressed his neck. "He's not breathing. Slow pulse." She began giving him CPR, leaning her weight against her hands atop each other in the center of Rex's breastbone and counting. After a series of compressions without any luck, she leaned down bringing her mouth close to his. "Damn it, Rex, breath." The pleading whisper didn't sound like her own.

A gush of intake fluttered against her lips. His eyes shot open, blinking several times. Then his lips went into that sexy, sideways grin that made her pants wet. "Were you gonna kiss me?" He winked.

She felt the beam on her face stretch from ear to ear. "I was going to blow some life into you." The man might be injured, but he smelled amazing. Like he'd stepped out of the shower, fresh and clean, with a hint of a woodsy fragrance she had recently grown to adore.

"Well? Are you going to kiss me? Or what?"

Her mouth met his with the gentlest glance her trembling body could manage. His lips were soft and tender, and she hated to pull away. "Rex, you were shot. We've got to stop the bleeding. Find the bullet wound."

A badge on the pleasant lady officer read, 'Office Izzy Comings.' She folded his vest over and pointed to the front. "I found it. No blood."

Bree eyed the red soaked fingers on her right hand. "But—"

Officer Comings snickered. "That's the big dude's blood."

Relief exhaled with a big 'O' from Bree's mouth. "So, Rex isn't shot?"

Izzy released the vest completely from Rex and laid it on the desktop. He grunted at the movement but didn't resist. She snickered. "Nope."

Rex's voice growled low and filled with pain. "Maybe not, but I think I was run over by a semi. Can you help me to my feet?"

"Chief," Izzy's hand shot up. "EMTs will be here in a few minutes. You should probably stay as you are."

"Nope. Not doing it." With Bree's help, he sat up. No choice. He was in motion, whether she supported him or not. "Son-of-a-bitch, that hurts." He jerked his head once, like he was trying to sling something into place.

Bree stroked a hand up and down his back. "You okay, Rex? You look a little pale. Maybe you should stay down."

"No, help me to the chair." He lifted his arms then slipped his feet beneath his big body. The women each put a shoulder beneath one arm, and he came to a standing position. "Whew, a bit lightheaded."

Izzy shoved the desk chair under his behind, and he plopped into it. Pulling Bree by the hand to stand so his side filled her with a warmth she welcomed. His arm slipped around her waist. Her quivering eased as his heat melted into her through the contact.

"You need a doctor, Rex." She slid a hand down his cheek and along his chin.

"Yeah, Chief. You really do." Izzy nodded then glanced toward the front entrance as two EMTs rushed inside with a gurney. She pointed to Burt. "Perpetrator down."

The male policeman stood to give them access to their patient. "Two slugs to the chest and a puncture to the right leg. Weapon is impaled intact."

They worked on Burt for a couple of minutes then lifted him onto the gurney, buckled him in, and pushed him out.

The male cop glanced at Rex. "I'll escort him to the hospital."

Rex nodded. "Good. I'll send Izzy over after this scene is contained, to help you out." The policeman with the nametag reading 'Officer Rusty Martin' followed the men through the front door.

A second set of EMTs raced in with their own gurney. Izzy waved them to where Rex sat. "Chief Ayers was shot. Round was stopped by protective gear. He's in pain, woozy, and his head hit the floor with a hard impact."

The women backed away so the responders could take care of Rex. The female copy extended her hand with a grin on her face. "Hi, I'm Izzy Comings. I've worked with the chief for a long time. You're the first woman he's ever mentioned. The man is totally into you."

Bree wanted to hug the woman, but they'd just met. Of course, the gal did just help save her life. "Thanks. I didn't realize he'd mentioned me to his…friends."

"You two stop gossiping over there." Rex spoke with a hoarse, protective growl, clearly afraid to put much muster into his voice for fear of causing himself more discomfort.

"It's not gossip when I'm the one we're talking about." Bree walked to stand behind him and put her hands on his shoulders.

Mya's face filled Bree's mind. "Rex, Burt's brother has Mya. I think they're at a hotel. He's going to hurt her if Burt doesn't call him before two a.m."

Rex shook his head. "Mya's fine. SWAT is taking her to my office now. The brother is in route to the hospital. Fired on an officer during the take down. Didn't go well for him."

Bree breathed the first normal breath since Rex had popped into sight. "Thank goodness. How did you know?"

Burt snickered. "My sister's kid works at their hotel. He called me when he saw Mya, wearing her pajamas, enter the hotel with the other man. I sent SWAT to retrieve her, and we came looking for you."

Bree gushed an exhale, and her shoulders relaxed. "I can hardly believe it. Thank goodness. It's over."

The uniformed man had taken Rex's pulse, blood pressure, and looked in his eyes. "No sign of concussion."

That was surprising. The way his head had hit the floor sounded like it would've cracked a bowling ball.

"Good thing Chief has a hard head." Izzy chuckled, thumbs in her utility belt.

Rex shot her a threatening glance that she took jokingly. The medical professional continued to probe around Rex's ribcage, finding obvious soreness. Rex blinked, and his cheeks rose and fell, but he said nothing. The emergency worker lifted Rex's shirt, exposing bright greens, purples, and blacks.

Bree gasped at the sight of his bruised torso. It was hard to believe something could color up so quickly.

Izzy's face quirked up. "Ouch, that's going to hurt."

"Already does." Rex twisted his lips sideways.

The man straightened. "You need ex-rays and a possible CT scan. Take a ride with us to the hospital, and let's get it over with."

Rex shook his head, nodding toward Bree. "No way. I'm taking this one to my office to see her aunt. I'll see to it later."

The guy gave him a sideways warning glare. "Later, as in before morning. Right?"

"Right." Rex groaned.

Bree stroked Rex's arm. "I'll personally see to it he goes to the hospital soon as we're done."

The guy reached for a pack of bandages. "Alright then. Let me tape you up, so you don't do any further harm. Can't have you piercing an internal organ with a broken rib. I'd venture to say you have a couple of them."

While the man bandaged Rex's injuries, he glanced around the room. "Izzy, go turn lights off and secure the premises. Then go on to the hospital to help Rusty with the perp. You two work out a schedule for guarding him until he can be released into custody. Let whoever is on duty at the front desk know before you get off tomorrow. These guys are not to be left alone. I don't know if they have accomplices or not." He pointed to his flak jacket. "Take this with you and turn it into evidence." She picked it up and threw it across her shoulder and set about following her boss's instructions.

Bree took Rex's hand, as the EMT's pushed their gurney out. It was cool in her own heated one. "I'm pretty sure they're alone in this. Burt was rather chatty."

Rex smiled; and pride caused those wrinkles she'd grown to love, form around his glorious eyes. "I believe you made quite an impression on your abductor. Nice to know you remain calm in an emergency."

CHAPTER TWENTY-SIX

Once they were alone, Bree strolled to the far set of shelves along the wall facing the kitchen. "Before we go, I should show you where James hid his stash." She turned to catch Rex's gaze.

He sat in the desk chair—the one James had died in a mere few days before. His brows went high. "You know…and you didn't relinquish it to your kidnapper, even when he threatened your life? Damn, woman, you've got nerves of steel." There was no anger in his voice, only admiration.

She smirked. "Don't kid yourself. I was quaking like an avalanche about to spill over and bury everything in its trail."

She spun her back toward him and began sliding her hands across shelving making up the entertainment center. Finding nothing she did the same to every space of the next shelf, which held a surround-sound speaker. Finding naught, she began examining the next lower shelf. Along the top of it in back, her fingers found their target. She pushed a hidden button.

With a click, the TV set swung outward to the left revealing a deep cubicle. A slim, right-side section held a laptop. She pulled it out and examined it. "I assume this is the missing computer."

Rex's chin rose. "I suppose so."

When he didn't reach for it, she returned it into its cubbyhole and ran a hand along the cool, slick metal of a bulky safe that took up most of the opening. "I'd wager James hid the cash in here."

"Yeah, probably. I'll get a lock expert over here tomorrow when we scour the house for evidence. This is a crime scene for the second time. We'll need to comb the house again for data to support the kidnapping trial."

She hadn't thought past tonight about what would happen to Burt and Zach. "No need. I know the combination. Or, at least, I think I do. Have you ID'd Burt and Zach?"

Rex grunted, sounding disappointed in himself. "Not yet, but we'll get it out of them once their conditions are stable."

She nodded somberly. "All I know is the one holding me is Burt. The guy who took Mya away was his younger brother Zach. Burt was a dock worker. Zach had worked at some sort of electronics store. Their dad was one of the many clients James stole from, also a dock worker. The dad's name is probably on the list of investors he swindled."

"I'll get a copy from the FBI tomorrow." Rex twisted uncomfortably looking in his seat.

"I have the list at home. I meant to turn it over to you tomorrow morning when I planned to bring you here to find the money. Lola Alessandra gave it to me. She got it from the Feds."

Rex looked confused, and his mouth flew open. "Lola Alessandra? Why does that name sound familiar?"

She smiled. "The mystery woman we saw James with. You must've done the research I suggested. Lola was James' lover in New York before he disappeared with the stolen funds."

Rex nodded, eyes shaded, as though he was putting data together like puzzle pieces for a clear mental picture. "Oh, yeah; that's it. You think they followed Ms. Alessandra here?"

"Burt told me they did."

"You certainly knew how to work old Burt, to get information out of him." Rex snickered.

She shrugged, turned, and plugged a few numbers into the safe's keypad. A click sounded. The door jarred slightly and opened. She pulled it wide. "Wow. So, that's what five-million dollars looks like."

Rex's brows went high. "I'd say it's more like somewhere near ten. Remember, the guy made a shitload of profit on selling plots and houses in this subdivision. I sure hope the FBI or SEC or whoever is responsible for determining what happens to this money, gives the profits to those poor folks James stole from. They deserve the benefit from his investment."

She should've known Rex would feel that way. "Exactly what I'm hoping for."

Rex pursed his lips. "That's out of our control. It's up to the powers that be. It's my job to provide the prosecutor with enough solid evidence and testimonies so he can nail these two kidnappers to the wall. They are going away until they're too old and frail to do anyone harm. They'll be charged with three counts of kidnapping. Assault with intent to kill. Manslaughter. Theft. Breaking and entering. Attempted murder of a police officer, and anything else we come up with."

She angled her head. "So, what do we do about it tonight?"

Rex tilted his chin toward her. "Lock it up securely. You and I are the only ones who know where it is. I'll take contact the Feds tomorrow and turn it over to whomever oversees the cash. For tonight, I'm going to reunite you with your aunt." He tried to stand, cringed, then sat back down.

She shut the safe and tried to reopen it to ensure it was locked. Then she pushed the television back into its position hearing the latch click. Strolling around the desk, she slid an arm around Rex. He stood with her help. As they strolled to the front exit, she flicked lights off and secured the front door.

She needed to drive. Rex was in no condition to do it. "My keys are in my bedroom. The car's in the garage."

"Let's take my truck. It's down the block that way." He nodded left, and she spotted his vehicle a few doors down.

She glanced at the sky. "It's a gorgeous night."

Rex's nose curled. "Pretty muggy, as usual for late summer."

She chuckled. "I must be getting used to the humidity."

Rex grinned. "Yep, I believe we're growing on you."

She snickered. "In more ways than you might guess."

Rex pulled his fob out and clicked the truck doors unlocked. "I sure hope so."

She led him to the passenger seat. "Get in. I'm driving." She opened the door, then tugged the keychain from his hand. He hesitated then released it. She waited while he got as comfortable as his condition allowed. Then she went to the driver's side.

When she was seat belted in, he studied her. "You sure you can manage a truck?"

She laughed out loud. "Listen, Chief, I've been driving tractors and trucks since I was ten years old. In the country, someone must drive the vehicle while stronger adults load hay in the field. So, the job usually goes to the biggest kid around. No worries. I never drove on the road back then."

He shook his head as though in wonder. "No worries. I should've known. You're a woman of many talents, Bree Collins."

Kicking the truck into gear she laughed. "And don't you forget it, Chief."

Rex took her hand, and it was as though it had found its true home.

CHAPTER TWENTY-SEVEN

At the police station Bree helped Rex to a chair in the bullpen then flew into Mya's arms. "Oh, Mya, I'm so happy to see you. I never thought we'd make it through this night. Was it awful? Are you okay? Did he hurt you?" She pulled back and looked Mya up and down.

Her precious aunt didn't look any worse for her wear. "I love you, Bree. I was terrified that big lug would hurt you...or worse. Are you alright?"

Bree nodded and stepped back. "I'm fine, but Rex may have some broken bones. He needs to see a doctor, but he insisted he needed to bring me here first...to see you."

Mya's brows tented with pity toward the chief. "Thank you, Rex. I appreciate it, but your health is important too."

Rex grinned from his chair. "No worries. I'll get medical attention later. I'm good for now."

It was a white lie, and they all knew it but let it go. Bree was overwhelmed with gratitude. "How are you, Mya?" Bree ran a hand down Mya's arm.

"I'm good. That man didn't hurt me. He just tied me to a chair in his hotel room. Then he flipped the television on to a game and began trying to consume every item in the minibar. I'm sure he intended to skip out on the hotel and not pay that bill. After a while, he went into the restroom. As he returned, zipping his trousers up, the SWAT team burst into the room from the door on one side and the window on the other. He was on the opposite end of the room from me, so I wasn't in much danger; but he panicked and fired on the officers. They shot him."

The young policeman at a desk Mya had been talking when they'd entered the room, stood. His nametag read Officer Van Carter. "Rusty just called. The perp at the hospital is out of surgery and under guard. The second is in surgery now."

Bree flexed. "That would be Burt. The first guy's name is Zach. They're brothers."

Carter wrote the names on a notepad. "Izzy texted a schedule for guarding the two perpetrators until they can be released into custody. I've scheduled officers to handle details."

Rex waved a hand toward Carter and to Bree's direction "Good work, Van. I assume you and Mya have made your acquaintances. This is her niece, Bree Collins."

Carter extended a hand, which Bree shook. "Nice finally meeting you, Ms. Collins. This joint's been buzzing about it ever since Chief met you. You've made quite an impression."

Rex groaned. "Does everyone in this precinct engage in idle gossip about coworkers? Is nothing sacred?"

Bree's insides were doing a happy jig. Everyone Rex knew seemed to know he and she had become a 'thing.' What kind of 'thing' were they, exactly? She could hardly wait to explore that question.

Studying Rex's face, she saw he was having a hard time breathing. "You're in pain and need some tender loving care."

He winked. "You volunteering?"

Heat flushed her face, but she was saved from having to answer when a couple of policemen strolled in, greeted everyone, and then took seats at their respective desks.

Rex glanced back to officer Carter, his voice weak and breathy. "Van, why don't you escort Ms. Landry home. Please check her house to ensure it's secure. If Mya wants, you can stick around and stand guard so she can get some rest."

"That won't be necessary." Mya put a hand up. "I should be fine once I'm sure my house is locked up and empty of unwanted guests." She glanced at Bree. "I'm calling a locksmith tomorrow and having all the locks upgraded and changed. "Officer Carter can help me get settled then go do more important work than babysitting me. I'll be fine, but I would appreciate the lift home." She glanced at Bree. "What about you, dear?"

Bree's gaze flicked to Rex then back. "I'm making sure this big fella gets medical care. Unless they handcuff him to a bed, he can see me home." She would wager that was the only way they'd get Rex to stay the night at the hospital.

Mya's brow shot up. "Maybe you should just see Rex to his home safely. He might need a bit of nursing. If you don't make it home tonight, I'll understand. You take care of your man."

My man? Was he? It sounded right. What did Rex think?

"Sounds like a plan to me." Rex didn't give her time to protest.

He struggled to his feet. Bree braced beneath his arm and slid hers around his slim waist, enjoying the scent of him so near and the feel of his strong muscles wrapped around her. He was warm. His heartbeat against her shoulder, provided a feeling of security and sensuality at the same time.

They hobbled as a unit, walking with Mya and Officer Carter to the parking lot. Mya kissed her cheek and strolled to Van's cruiser.

The sky was lit like a dark sea of sparkling diamonds. A half-moon hung casually to the right, as though having witnessed nothing unusual occurring below. Cool night air had a tint of river scent in its heady odor. City night sounds differed from where she'd grown up in the eastern mountains, but she was growing accustomed to their peculiarities. Bree's world might've been in turmoil, but the rest of the universe continued like any other night.

Life goes on. Some things changed. Others never did.

She was but a tiny gleam in the vastness of eternity. Bree and Mya would heal from their trauma and be stronger for having experienced it. Burt and Zach would live out their desperate lives behind bars, never to enjoy the fruits of their father's hard labor.

Wrongs would be righted, and lives of the injured would heal.

Rex's wounds would mend. He held a tight grip around her shoulders telling her he needed more than her physical support. They were meant to be together. Not just for tonight.

THE END

DEAR READER,

If you liked the *Fresh Starts, Dirty Money*, I'm sure you're going to love reading more from Lynda Rees. Here's a sample to get you started.

FLIP OR FLOP,
MURDER HOUSE
CHAPTER 1

Charli Owens strode a few feet from her pickup to where the auction would be held. A few characters she knew casually waited for the Sheriff and County Clerk to exit the Sweetwater courthouse. A couple of insurance agents, a boring, grey-suited guy studying his clip board—a bank representative monitoring the sale, and an older couple, made up the group.

A pickup truck with ladder racks on top pulled to the curb and stopped. Buckets and equipment filled the bed—a contractor's work vehicle. A too-hot-to-be-loose on the street guy stepped out of the driver's side and rounded the truck.

Trouble.

Shaggy blonde hair draped his neck, framing a swoon-worthy face. Light eyes glowed from his smile, noticeable from the distance. It lit up his face, causing adorable wrinkles at their sides. A slim waist joined long, slender legs in tight-fitting jeans. He dwarfed the petite, blonde with cropped locks, who climbed from the passenger side. The female reached in and helped a miniature version of her out.

Bouncing red curls topped the toddler's head, and she wore overall blue jeans with a red tee shirt. Her father took her hand. The mom tiptoed to kiss his cheek, bent to do the same to their daughter then strolled around, jumping into the driver's seat then sped away.

Lovely family. No danger there.

A pang hit Charli's heart, having hoped to have a household like that by now.

Hunky Daddy ambled slowly, so his daughter could keep up as they walked. Petite like her mother, the imp looked about four or five. Dad stood six-feet-four inches tall at least, probably more like six-foot-six. Broad shoulders strained fabric of his black tee stretching across a rolling chest and rippling abs.

Stopping at the rock wall by the courthouse steps, he squatted and whispered to the little one. She slipped behind him, and tiny arms surrounded his neck. He grasped the pudgy hands, lifted her onto his back then positioned himself to allow her to step onto the wall. She sat with legs dangling. He hopped to land beside her and put an arm across her shoulders, giving her a sweet hug.

Charli pushed away jealousy gnawing at her and waltzed toward a familiar couple. "Hi, Sandy, Mike. Are you looking to buy?"

Twenty-something Mike Carey shook her hand. "Not sure we're in position to purchase at auction."

Sandy Carey slid a palm across her protruding tummy and shook Charli's hand "Mike and I don't understand the process."

Mike nodded. "We decided to observe, though we'd love to bid on the Blossom Lane house."

Charli swallowed a lump lodged in her throat. "You aren't swayed by—"

Mike interrupted her bumbling attempt at posing the question tactfully. "Not a bit. It had nothing to do with us."

Charli exhaled relief and inhaled hope, nodding at Sandy's belly. "Congratulations, I didn't realize you were expecting. Is that why you're in the market?" There was the green-eyed monster again. Charlie pushed it down.

Sandy beamed. "Our daughter is coming in September. We've prequalified for an FHA mortgage, but there's nothing on the market we're interested in. Blossom would fit us well, but we're not sure about tackling a fixer upper."

Mike's faced reddened. "I'm not helpless, but a lot needs to be done to that house. You're an expert and a real estate agent. Maybe you can help." He pulled out a paper and handed it to Charli. "This is our mortgage approval letter."

Relieved she wouldn't need to compete with the young couple for the property, she reviewed the document then handed it to Mike. "You won't be able to purchase a house needing renovation. FHA strenuously inspects your purchase to ensure it won't require major improvements for a long while. They don't want to put you in a position where they might need to foreclose."

Mike solemnly nodded. "I was afraid of that."

Charli smiled warmly. "I'm bidding on that property for my next rehab."

Sandy frowned. "Don't you remodel more expensive houses?"

Charli put a happy face on. "I'm taking the company in a different direction. There's a vast market for reasonably priced housing." They didn't need to know about Charli's effort to salvage her company and make a mark on her own.

Mike folded the sheet and stuck it in his pocket. "We're having trouble finding a suitable home."

"If I'm successful and get Blossom Lane, my intention is to bring it to perfect condition. I'll give you first crack at it if you want."

Sandy's eyes grew wide. "Yes, absolutely, we want to take a look when you're ready."

Mike grinned at his wife then turned to Charli. "Thank you. That would be perfect."

Charli cocked her head and eyed the handsome father and his child. She had hoped to be the only contractor bidding. "Pray I win at auction."

The strange man's head lifted, allowing a better view of his face. A square jaw eased into a grin, showing off glistening whites. Amusement appeared in almost iridescent gray eyes. Tiny wrinkles formed on outsides as he nodded pleasantly in Charli's direction.

Damn. She'd been caught gawking. Just what a good-looking guy needed, a stroke to his ego.

The antique, double doors opened. Sheriff Wyatt Gordon stepped out with a woman. He scanned and welcomed the crowd, introduced himself and the clerk and explained the process. The auction began.

An agent Charli recognized purchased a couple of city plots for his out-of-town insurance company. Bidding started for a laundromat. The older couple upped the banker's offer. A man in a business suit made a competing proposal. They countered a couple of times until he gave a resolved shake of his head.

Hunky Daddy sat quietly observing. That didn't bode well in Charli's mind. She'd hoped to avoid competition. His vehicle screamed contractor, someone who might bid against her. Blossom was the only property left.

Charli took a final look at figures in her notebook, reminding herself to stay within budget. She'd carefully inspected the house earlier in the week, gotten accurate pricing data together and assessed renovated value based on market data. Her bottom dollar was enough to satisfy the mortgage holder. It might not stand up against an aggressive bidder.

This guy better not be here for her house. The place had good bones. She needed it to keep her company afloat but didn't have money to get into a bidding war, not if she planned to keep a cushion to deal with unforeseen issues.

It wasn't simply her need to eat and provide shelter for her family. Self-esteem had suffered a deafening blow during dissolution of her partnership. Her pride was the size of a two-penny nail.

Damn it to hell.

That son of a bitch, Thompson Shade, wasn't about to end her. Shoulders rocked back. Her chin shot high. Resolve eased her rigid jaw.

She'd bought many a house at auction, designed, remodeled and successfully sold million-dollar residences at major profits. This dinky, three-bedroom pit wasn't about to get the better of her.

Wyatt opened the bid. The bank rep's hand shot up. The elderly couple upped the price a thousand dollars. Charli's hand went high, accepting the auctioneer's offer a thousand more. Next submission increased another grand. Hunky Daddy's mitt rose into the air. Charli took the next grand. The old couple's eyes met, and they dropped out. Hunky Daddy and Charli went up a thousand a time, playing against each other.

Charli gaped at her scratchpad. She lifted her paw and shouted a proposition five-thousand dollars higher. Hunky Daddy grimaced then shrugged as he shook his head.

Wyatt's announced, "Sold to Charli Owens."

Relief flooded her lungs and swilled into her gut. She smiled pleasantly toward Hunky Daddy.

He'd already hopped down and was lifting his child to her feet. Without a gaze Charli's direction, he took the girl's hand; and they strolled from Town Square.

His fine ass moved side-to-side. Broad shoulders shifted with ease of his stride, as those lengthy legs took him and his daughter down the street. Sandy, shaggy hair was chin length and might look lazy on some men but enhanced sex appeal to a peak on this guy. She sighed when they rounded the corner and disappeared.

With nothing left to watch, Charli waltzed into the courthouse to finalize the deal. She'd searched the title, having done it many times before. Paying cash, the title company was prepared to close in three days.

Afterward on the street, Charli whipped out her phone and dialed. Her best gal pal, Jaiden. "So? Did you get it?" Deputy Jaiden Coldwater's Texas drawl was nearly identical to local, Kentucky twang.

Charli chuckled. "Yep, I figured Wyatt would've filled you in."

"Nope, information is confidential until closing. The boss said if you wanted me to know, you'd tell me. Congratulations. Your business is on track. We need to celebrate and then find you a decent fella. You need to get that fine tush of yours back out there." Since Jaiden had gotten engaged to handsome surgeon, Clay Barnes, she'd been on a mission to fix Charli up.

Charli's eyes shot toward the heavens. "Hell no; I've sworn off the male sex, at least until I finish this rehab and sell the property."

"Whatever you say, but you can't stay off the market for long. Your love life needs a total rebuild."

"Don't I know it. The finest male specimen I've seen in a long time showed up at the sale today. The dude was eye candy, palpitation worthy and sweating testosterone clear across the courthouse lawn. It literally made my thong wet when his dreamy peepers met mine. I was perspiring blood; my face went so red."

"You don't sound sure about this temporary-celibate thing." Jaiden chuckled. She hadn't masked her relief when Thompson had tossed Charli aside like yesterday's takeout, and she wasn't on board with Charli's *no men for a while* choice.

"Honey, I'm not dead. There's nothing wrong with my sight. I might not be shopping, but I can view the merchandise. That boy was too hot to ignore. I had to soak up some of that sex appeal while he was hanging around. I can tell you my libido is fully intact."

"So why didn't you hit that?"

Charli tucked away in her mind the male vision causing her to perspire like the morning dew. "The guy is taken, married. They have the most adorable, little girl."

"Got 'cha," Jaiden groaned. "Oh well, at least, what's his name hasn't ruined you for other men. There's a deserving, guy out there for you, Charli. You'll find him when you're ready. Speaking of ready, when are we going to celebrate?"

AUTHOR'S NOTE:

Get *Flip or Flop, Murder House* at
https://www.lyndareesauthor.com
For more from this author, consult the list of
published books in the following pages.

I hope you enjoy my work and we become life-long friends. Please join my **VIP** group.

Get the latest book **deals, exclusive content**, and **FREE** reads by joining my **VIPs**. Email for a **FREE** copy of *Leah's Story* at
https://preview.mailerlite.com/t1a6j6
Website: http://www.lyndareesauthor.com
Email: lyndareesauthor@gmail.com

Lynda Rees
The Murder Guru©
Love is a dangerous mystery. Enjoy the ride!©

BOOKS BY LYNDA REES

Historical Romance:
> *Gold Lust Conspiracy*

Mystery:

> ***The Bloodline Series:***
> *Leah's Story*
> *Parsley, Sage, Rose, Mary & Wine*
> *Blood & Studs*
> *Hot Blooded*
> *Blood of Champions*
> *Bloodlines & Lies*
> *Horseshoes & Roses*
> *The Bloodline Trail*
> *Real Money*
> *The Bourbon Trail*

Reggie Chronicles:
> *Hart's Girls, #1*
> *Heart of the Matter, #2*
> *Magnolia Blossoms, #3*

Single Titles:
> *God Father's Day*
> *Madam Mom*
> *2nd Chance Ranch*
> *Flip or Flop, Murder House*
> *Fresh Start, Dirty Money*

7 Book Anthology: *Sacrifice For Love:*
> *Second Chance Romance*, Lynda Rees

Children's Middle Grade:
> *Freckle Face & Blondie*
> *The Thinking Tree*

Children's PictureBooks:
> *NO FEAR*
> *No Fear Learning and Activity Book*

Find information about these books at website:
http://www.lyndareesauthor.com

Fresh Starts, Dirty Money

ABOUT LYNDA REES

Lynda Rees, The Murder Guru, is a storyteller, an award-winning novelist, and a free-spirited dreamer with workaholic tendencies and a passion for writing.

A diverse background, visits to exotic locations, and curiosity about how history effects today's world fuels her writing. Born in the splendor of the Appalachian Mountains as a coal miner's daughter and part-Cherokee, she grew up in northern Kentucky when Newport prospered as a mecca for gambling and sin.

Lynda's work is published in cozy mystery, historical romance, romantic suspense, middle-grade mystery, children's picture books, non-fiction, and self-help non-fiction.

Fresh Starts, Dirty Money

MADE IN U. S. A.
© 2023
SWEETWATER PUBLISHING COMPANY

CPSIA information can be obtained
at www.ICGtesting.com
Printed in the USA
BVHW041818030523
663527BV00003B/69